Dedicated to the Glory
of God the Father, the
Son and the Holy Spirit

To - BRIAN

Grace and Peace of our Lord
be with you always.

Jimmy

1

My Vision:

I asked the Lord…..

"And the Lord answered me and said, write the vision, and make it plain on tablets, so he who reads it may run with the message. For still the vision awaits its appointed time; it hastens to the end-it will not lie. If it seems slow, wait for it; it will surely come, it will not delay." Habakkuk 2: 2

Biblical Theology

God's ultimate purpose in redemptive history is to create a people to dwell in His presence, glorifying Him through numerous varied activities and enjoying Him forever. The story begins with God in eternal glory and ends with God and His people in eternal glory. At the center stands the cross where God revealed His glory through His son.

The Biblical story of redemption must be understood within the larger story of creation. First Adam, and later Israel, was placed in God's sanctuary (the Garden and the Promised Land respectively), but both Adam and Israel failed to be faithful, obedient stewards, and both were expelled from the sanctuary God had created for them. But Jesus Christ, the second Adam, the son of Abraham, the son of David, was faithful and obedient to God. Though the world killed him, God raised him to life, which meant that death was defeated. Through his Spirit, God pours into sinners the resurrection life of his Son creating a new humanity in Christ. Those who are in Christ move through death into new life and exaltation in God's sanctuary, there enjoy His presence forever.

Source: The Bookends of Biblical Theology|ESV.org

First letter of Paul to the Corinthians
1 Corinthians 2:1-2

When I came to you, brethren, I did not come with superiority of speech or of wisdom, proclaiming to you the testimony of God. For I determined to know nothing among you except Jesus Christ, and Him crucified.

It does not matter if our testimony is simple or forcefully effective. If Jesus is the center of the testimony, it will plant the seed that the Holy Spirit will nourish your testimony.

Your witness; your testimony; can make the difference in someone spending eternity in heaven or hell.

Prologue

If you will permit, I would like to tell you a three way love story between Michael, Jen and God. It is a story about the life of a six year old boy and a man's journey from darkness to light that takes him into the depths of hell, only to return by the grace of God. The story is laced throughout with passages from the Holy Bible. I hope you enjoy "From Darkness to Light."

Jimmy Campagna

2017

Chapter One: The Beginning

"Better is the end of a thing than the beginning thereof; and the patient in spirit is better than the proud in spirit." Ecclesiastes 7:8

The sun gradually began its descent below the Georgia horizon as Michael Tillman played in the backyard. The bright autumn leaves rustled with a gentle breeze as their colors intermingled with the rays of the setting sun. The Augusta countryside was silent, apart from the laughter of the young boy echoing across the meadow. The last normal day of Michael's life was slowly coming to a close.

Behind him, the house he had lived in for the entire six years of his life stood tall against the rural landscape, a comforting sight and the only existence Michael had ever known.

On the back porch steps sat the Tillman's maid, Matty, shelling peas and watching Michael play. She smiled to herself as she watched him jump around in the waning daylight. Matty had known the Tillman family for years, taking care of Michael's father, Terry, when he was a child. Not having a family of her own, Terry and Michael had been like her own children for as long as she could remember.

Terry had grown up in a similar setting to Michael, his father being a prominent judge in Valdosta, as well as the president of a powerful political and financial conglomerate known as the Enterprise. To say that Terry came from an affluent household would be an understatement. Judge Tillman was considered the most powerful man in Valdosta, if not all of South Georgia.

Matty had been hired by the Judge when she was only twenty-one years old, a job that she would keep for the next eighteen years. When Terry left the Judge's farm to go to law school and to marry Susan, Matty had expected to be unemployed. Instead, she was pleasantly surprised when they asked her to accompany them to Augusta. She had jumped at the opportunity to join them while Susan attended medical school.

Along with Matty, the couple had hired an older woman named Ms. Broadwick, who looked after the Tillman estate as their housekeeper.

Most days Matty stayed home, taking care of Michael by herself, as Terry and Susan worked late into the night. Terry was a hard-working attorney, and Matty could not help but be impressed by his ambition.

Now, as she sat watching Michael in the backyard, she couldn't help but think of how much he reminded her of Terry. He was such a kind boy, with a wit that far surpassed his young age. This was due largely to the fact that the Tillman's had hired a personal tutor, Mr. Thomson, to teach the boy privately five days a week. Over the course of two years, Michael had been taught everything from arithmetic to reading and writing.

At first, Matty had thought a tutor unnecessary, but after seeing the great strides Michael had made in a matter of weeks, she quickly came to appreciate Mr. Thomson. Michael was extremely advanced for a child of his age. However, he seldom interacted with other children, as he had no brothers and sisters and no friends. In fact, Matty was probably the only friend he really had. After all, he saw her much more than he saw anyone else, even his parents.

Even now, Matty and Michael hadn't seen Terry and Susan for several days, as they had taken a weeklong trip to the countryside. Matty didn't mind though. Nothing brought her more joy than spending time with Michael.

Matty had come so far since Terry's childhood, and she wouldn't give up her job with the Tillmans for anything in the world.

The sound of Michael's voice startled her from her thoughts.

"Matty," he called across the yard. "Who's that?"

She looked up from the bowl of peas to see a car screeching down the long gravel driveway toward the Tillman house, leaving a cloud of dust in its path. She wasn't expecting Terry and Susan home for another two days, and they rarely got visitors.

Matty stood up and called Michael back to the house, ushering him into the kitchen as she glanced over her shoulder at the car steadily approaching. She lingered for a moment in the doorway, finally realizing that it was a police car. She waited in the kitchen for several minutes, brushing the dirt off of Michael's clothes and listening as Ms. Broadwick opened the door to the police officers.

Whatever was happening, she knew it couldn't be good. Her heart sank when she heard Ms. Broadwick's voice in the adjoining room.

"Oh no. Oh my goodness. No! No!" Ms. Broadwick cried.

Picking Michael up with shaky hands and setting him on a stool, Matty told him to stay in the kitchen and she would be right back.

When Matty reached the front door, she saw the housekeeper with both hands over her face, crying and shaking her head back and forth.

"Wh…What's going on," Matty breathlessly asked the officer closest to her.

"The boy's parents have been in an accident," the officer replied hesitantly. "They were both killed… I'm so sorry."

Matty gasped, clutching her heart and sinking to her knees.

"The Judge, Mr. Tillman's father, has been notified," the officer continued despite her sobs. We also contacted Doctor Tillman's sister Catherine. Both of them will be in touch with you soon regarding the boy."

Matty nodded her head as tears streaked down her face and fell through her fingers. The police officers politely continued issuing their report, though Matty heard little of what they said.

What would she tell Michael? Where would he go?

After finishing with their report, the officers slipped out of the house, offering their condolences and leaving Mrs. Broadwick and Matty alone in the foyer.

It wasn't long before Catherine Atkins, Susan's unmarried sister, drove up the driveway. Matty wiped her eyes with the back of her hands, trying to hide her distress from Michael. Walking into the kitchen, she told him that his Aunt Catherine was here and she wanted to talk to him.

Catherine came into the kitchen a few minutes later. Michael could see that she had been crying. She dabbed at her puffy eyes with a handkerchief, stifling a sob as she laid eyes on her young nephew.

"It's alright Michael," she began. "Everything is going to be alright." Catherine shook her head and took a deep breath. "Do you know who God is, Michael?"

The question caught the young boy off guard. With everyone acting so strange he wasn't expecting that to be the first thing his aunt asked him.

"Yes," Michael replied. "Mama said God is a spirit."

"Well, your Mama and Daddy have gone to be with God in heaven," Catherine said, almost in a whisper. She waited a minute for her words to sink in. From the look on the boy's face though, she could tell he did not understand.

"But when will they come home," Michael asked, his confusion turning into frustration.

"Michael, they are not coming home. They have gone to be with God forever." At this, Catherine broke down in tears.

"Why didn't they take me? Didn't they want me anymore?" Michael turned and said, "Matty, why are you crying?"

Matty said, "Come Michael, you have to take a bath and get cleaned up."

Within an hour, Matty received a call from Judge Tillman. Although she had worked for the Judge for many years, Matty felt like she barely knew him. She had been told time and again of his prestige and power throughout Valdosta, but she had had little contact with him despite living in his home for eighteen years. He had been extremely elusive as a parent to Terry, and she couldn't help but feel as if there was something mysterious in the way he ran his household.

Now, as she sat clutching the telephone to her ear, the sound of his voice brought back a flood of memories from so many years before. "Matty, listen to everything I tell you," began the Judge brusquely." He was never one for formalities. "In a few hours two men will arrive at the house. They are lawyers and they will take care of all the details and legal matters; you don't have to bother with anything. If there is a problem or if you have any questions, they are there to handle everything."

Matty could tell he was distraught. He sounded frantic and distracted, nothing like his usually confident bravado.

"The lawyers have a check for Ms. Broadwick. This should compensate her for six months' salary. She is to be dismissed of her duties immediately; do you understand?"

"Yes sir," Matty replied.

"There will be another car arriving soon with a few of my men," he continued. "They are there to pack all of Terry and Susan's belongings. Tell Ms. Catherine to take anything of Susan's she wants, and everything else is to be packed and ready to be put in a moving truck that will be there at about noon tomorrow. Now Matty, I want you to come to the Farm again and live with me and my wife, to look after and help raise Michael. The moving truck will be at the house to bring whatever you want, so don't worry about the finances. Everything will be paid. I want you, Michael, and the lawyers to come back when they are ready. Matty, I want you down here. You are the only person in this world that Michael has, and he needs you. I will pay you whatever is necessary."

Matty wiped a tear from her face and replied, "You don't have to

pay me nothin'. I could never live
without Michael. He is all I have."

The lawyers, Matty and Michael
left Augusta two days later. Matty
was excited when they drove up the
driveway to the beautiful antebellum
house she had lived in many years
before. The house was built prior to
the war between the states, about
1845. The Tillman house was one of
three plantation houses in Valdosta
still standing. "The Farm", as it
was called, was handed down for
generations. Located six miles from
the city limits, the Tillman estate
stood at the end of a long dirt road
bordered by two-hundred year old oak
and pine trees. The ground around
the farm was covered in palmetto
bushes and vines, and two cypress
ponds with Spanish moss hanging from
the trees, added to the spectacle
that many people admired.

When the car pulled into the
front of the house, the Judge and
his wife Emily were there to meet
them. They hugged Michael and told
him how much he would like living
there.

"Oh Michael, you're simply going to love it here," his grandmother cried, forcing herself to sound upbeat, though she was utterly heartbroken over the loss of her son.

"We have a swimming pool, fishing ponds, and lots of horses." She continued to talk though Michael heard little of what she said. The Farm was the last place he wanted to be right now.

He wanted to be in heaven with his Mama and Daddy. Why did God have to take them away?

He hated God.

Chapter 2: A Friend

"A man of many companions may come to ruin, but there is a friend who sticks closer than a brother." Proverbs 18:24

Although Michael attempted to hide his disdain for the Farm, it was quickly obvious to Matty that he hated his new home. His normally cheerful persona was replaced with a sullen expression that seldom left his face, despite the fun, new activities the Farm had to offer.

He refused to feed the horses or chickens, and he wouldn't gather eggs or vegetables from the garden.

The Judge and his wife would seldom discipline him, and as a result, he became more and more unruly as the months progressed. As usual, Matty was the first to notice the change in Michael's behavior, voicing her concerns to the Judge on several occasions. However, the Judge was a busy man and simply told her not to worry about it. "Michael needs to live his own life and make decisions for himself," the Judge would retort each time Matty confronted him. "After all, his behavior is to be expected considering the trauma he has recently endured." Matty was concerned for the boy's well-being but she knew it was not her place to discipline him. Despite Matty's warnings, the Tillmans continued to spoil him excessively, though he was never satisfied with his grandparents' gifts.

Weeks after they had arrived at the Farm, Matty reflected on the drastic change in Michael's character after such a short period of time. Michael had become very hard to deal with. He was completely different from the boy she had loved and taken care of not long before.

The summer quickly ended and Michael entered the first grade. Thanks to his tutor, he was much more advanced in his studies than the other students. However, the school staff felt it necessary to keep Michael with children of his own age, since he had had little contact with other boys and girls growing up.

Each quarter, Michael was given additional, more advanced books to study in class so that he wouldn't get bored.

Although Michael had no trouble in the classroom, his interaction with the other students was a totally different matter. Michael had never played with children his own age, and this was quickly obvious to the other kids on the playground. After living with his grandparents for several months, it never occurred to him that he couldn't have everything the way he wanted it, and this attitude didn't sit well with his classmates.

The next few years went by much the same as the first year. However, one day when Michael was nine years old, the boys chose sides to play baseball. Michael was chosen by one team and told to play in the right field. As the game progressed, a ball was hit directly toward him, rolling past as everyone yelled at him to throw the ball into the infield. The boy who hit the ball quickly rounded the bases and scored a run, while Michael fumbled with the glove on his hand.

With the other kids screaming at him, he threw the glove on the ground in frustration and stormed off the field. Fuming, he marched to the bleachers on the verge of tears.

He had never played baseball a day in his life, Michael told himself. How could they possibly expect him to know what to do?

The sound of footsteps in the dirt stirred him from his melancholy, as another boy approached from the field. The boy boldly walked up beside him and sat down. Michael had seen him before, but never talked to him. He seldom talked to the other children, most of them avoided him anyway.

However, as he looked up into the boy's bright blue eyes, there was something different there that he had never seen in the eyes of the other children – a sort of concern, as if he was worried about Michael.

They sat in silence for a second, as Michael waited for the boy to speak first. "My name is Billy Dean," he said, as if it should mean something to Michael. "You wanna be my friend?"

"Do you think I need a friend?" Michael seethed.

"No, I don't think you need a friend," Billy replied. "I need a friend."

Michael hadn't expected Billy to answer like that. As he looked into the boy's friendly eyes, there was a part of him that couldn't help but feel sorry for Billy. Although Michael found it hard to trust the other boys, he believed everything that Billy told him. He didn't know why, but he could tell that Billy was genuinely interested in being his friend.

"Alright, I'll be your friend."

It didn't take long for Michael to realize that, other than needing a friend, he and Billy Dean really had very little in common. Billy was the poorest kid in the class, while Michael's family was by far the wealthiest. Thus, the boys' upbringings had been extremely different.

The first time Billy spent the night at Michael's house he was stunned by the environment he was introduced to. It was as if he had stepped into a completely different world, full of running water, gourmet food, and luxurious beds. Before long, Billy was spending most nights at the Tillman estate. It was unlike anything he could have ever imagined, especially considering where he had grown up.

Billy's home was located several miles from Michael's house, down an old dirt road in the poorer section of east Valdosta. Only two miles from the Okefenokee Swamp, the Dean home was merely a ramshackle building in the middle of the woods.

Billy lived with his mother, Janet Dean, on about forty acres of land that she inherited from her husband, after he had been shot and killed in a bar room brawl. The land had been in the Dean family for generations.

Michael considered Billy's house nothing but a shack, but enjoyed going over nonetheless. The change of atmosphere was refreshing to him, especially when the boys began exploring the swamp. The swamp offered a variety of new animals and landscapes of which Billy was very knowledgeable.

The next summer, when Michael and Billy were eleven years old, one of Billy's uncles gave him an old cypress built John Boat along with a five horse power motor. The motor had lost much of its power, but it was better than paddling. Billy had been going into the swamp with his uncles and cousins for as long as he could remember. Most of the Deans lived in Folkston, a small town at the edge of the swamp. Billy had grown up around the swamp and knew every gator trail, every pond and every small island. The first few times Billy took Michael into the swamp, he sat in the back of the boat so he could guide them through the narrow gator trails. As Billy floated along, they would see gators on the islands, sunning themselves, and sometimes as the boat passed too close, a gator or two would slide into the water beside them.

Billy would point out the various life forms as they journeyed deeper and deeper into the swamp. Sometimes they would stop and walk on an island, and the island would shake as they walked over it. Billy would grab hold of a tree and pull it back and forth, as the island rocked under their feet. This is why the Seminole Indians named the swamp Okeefenokee – the land of the trembling earth, he had explained.

Billy also taught Michael about the wildlife; there were turtles, beavers, frogs, lizards, and larger animals like the bobcat, coyote, bear or white tailed deer. He told Michael about a large number of birds such as the yellow billed slider, egrots, herrons, wood storks, and sandhill crains.

Billy even showed Michael a type of herb whose leaves repelled mosquitoes.

Michael became enamored by the swamp, so much so that he wanted to spend all his spare time there. The new landscape intrigued him, giving him the opportunity to learn so much that he had never even considered at the Farm.

One day in early July, Billy took him deep into the swamp to an island with an old dilapidated cabin. His uncles and cousins had somewhat restored it, making it at least good enough for shelter. When they had first discovered the cabin, they had found a variety of copper containers, a rusted kettle, and a few broken jars. Billy told Michael that they were almost certain it had been built for a moonshine still.

The swamp was relatively quiet in the day, except for the occasional bird call or screech of a wildcat. But in the evening, the swamp came alive, echoing with the calls of hundreds of animals, big and small.

As much as the swamp interested Michael, Billy took the same level of interest in the Tillman Farm. Built with pine beams, the antebellum style home stood in stark contrast to the house Billy had grown up in. As one of the only homes of the early nineteenth century still intact, the Tillman estate was somewhat of a rare sight, especially to people as downtrodden as Billy's family.

Although Michael preferred the swamp and Billy the Farm, it made no difference to the boys where they stayed, as long as they were together. It was in those summer days of their youth that their bond grew increasingly tighter.

It was about this time in his childhood that the Judge began to take an interest in what Michael learned, not at school but on the Farm. He thought it necessary that Michael be taught how to hunt, fish and ride horses. He also began to instruct him on driving his old Jeep around the estate and running the motor boat around the Tillman's ponds.

Above everything, the Judge wanted the boy to learn to look after himself in every way that he could. Though he was only a child, he thought it was extremely important for the boy to possess a certain level of independence.

As Michael became better friends with Billy, the new boy began to learn these new skills alongside Michael.

Despite his instruction, the Judge quickly came to the conclusion that Michael was not as tough as he should be. Stooping down and looking him in the eye with a stern gaze, the Judge would tell him, "If you want to ever be successful in life, you must learn to take what you want instead of waiting for it to be given to you. Rules are made for those who accept them. They are not made for us…Remember that."

Michael would never forget the words of his grandfather.

At school, Michael's behavior began to change to conform to the Judge's philosophy of aggression. The other boys quickly targeted him for his spoiled attitude, resenting him for the arrogance he portrayed wherever he went.

After Michael insulted another boy on the playground, he was punched in the nose and knocked to the ground, humiliated in front of his classmates. Stumbling home on the verge of tears, Michael collapsed before the Judge who was furious over the incident. Michael was sure his grandfather was just as angry at him for not fighting back as he was at the other boy who had punched him to begin with.

The next day, the Judge introduced Michael to a man he had hired to train him in self-defense. "Michael, this is Mr. Harris," his grandfather stated. "He'll teach you to fight for yourself. I expect you will cooperate." Before leaving the room, the Judge turned to Mr. Harris and bluntly stated, "I expect him never to lose a fight again." With that, he left Michael in the hands of his instructor who continued to teach him week after week.

Michael didn't think the training was necessary but he didn't dare question his grandfather's decision. Day after day, the trainer instructed Michael, showing him how to punch, kick, and wrestle his way out of every situation imaginable.

Several weeks later, Michael confronted the boy who had punched him. Grabbing him by the collar, Michael threw the boy to the ground as he screamed in protest. Springing up, the boy plowed into Michael. In a matter of seconds, both boys were on the ground, punching and kicking each other as they rolled in the concrete. It didn't take long for Michael to gain the upper hand, giving the boy a bloody nose as the other boys struggled to break up the fight. Pulling Michael away, his teacher took the boy with the bloody nose to the nurse's office.

Michael had finally won.

The Judge was right, he did have the power to get anything he wanted. He just had to take it.

Chapter 3: Trouble

When Michael was thirteen, he entered the seventh grade and was confronted with a new bully, a boy named Beau Brock. Beau had failed his last two attempts at the seventh grade, and at fifteen years old, he towered above the other boys. Beau quickly became the school bully, particularly finding an interest in Michael. One day, as Michael chased Billy around the school yard, Beau stuck out his foot sending Michael tumbling into the dirt. As Michael hit the ground, he felt the breath escape his lungs. Gasping for air, Michael jumped to his feet, propelled by the rage that quickly overshadowed his pain.

Beau smirked, proudly sauntering away, only to be swept off his feet as Michael plowed into him from behind. Before the older boy could react, Michael was on top of him, biting, clawing, and kicking as if his life depended on it. In a matter of seconds, the teachers grabbed Michael by the shoulders and lifted him off of Beau.

"Don't you ever mess with me again," Michael cried as he and Beau were dragged by their shirts to the principal's office.

Badly bruised and lips bleeding, Beau managed to smirk at him again, enraging Michael all the more.

Five minutes later, both boys sat in the office of Principal Wensel Moore, a small, weak man with horn-rimmed glasses. His thin face vaguely resembled that of a goat, making it hard for the boys to take him too seriously.

Instead of a scolding as the boys had expected, Principal Moore grabbed a paddle from the shelf behind his desk and quietly gestured both boys forward. Telling the boys to bend over, he swatted each of them fifteen times. Michael's face burned red, though now from humiliation instead of rage.

With the paddling out of the way, Principal Moore motioned for them to take their seats again.

"Boys," he began in a squeaky voice, not much louder than a whisper, "I expect better from the two of you. As much as it pains me, you leave me no choice but to suspend you from school for the next week for your unruly conduct. You may go… and when you return to school, I expect better behavior from both of you."

Michael was shocked. He had never been disciplined in such a way in his entire life. And to top it all off, he had been suspended from school. Hadn't the Judge taught him to fight for himself in such situations?

When Michael returned home, he told the Judge everything, from the fight, to the paddling, to his suspension. When he finished the story, he saw an unusual fire in his grandfather's eyes.

"I…I'm sorry," Michael stammered, unsure of what else to say.

"Come with me," the Judge seethed.

Taking him strongly by the arm, the Judge put him in the car, and drove him back to school without saying another word, quietly fuming as they pulled into the school's parking lot.

Michael's heart thudded loudly inside his chest as his grandfather marched through the front door, down the hall, and into Principal Moore's office. The Judge charged around the desk and grabbed the mousy old administrator.

"Don't you ever lay a hand on my grandson again," he screamed. "If you ever touch him again, you will answer to me. I will pull you out of here, tie you to the flag pole, and give you a proper wuppin' in front of the entire school if I have to. Do you understand me!"

Michael had never seen his grandfather like this before, red faced and livid. He was starting to worry that he would actually harm Mr. Moore.

The principal stammered incoherently as he tried frantically to pull away from the man towering over him. The Judge finally released him, and Mr. Moore fell into his seat, trembling from head to toe.

"As for Michael's suspension," continued the Judge, "I want him back in school tomorrow! As for the other boy, I expect him to be expelled from this school for good. That boy is too old and simply a trouble maker. Get rid of him immediately!"

Satisfied that he had gotten his point across, the Judge grabbed Michael by the hand and led him out the door, without receiving a response from Mr. Moore, who stared forward with wide eyes.

Michael was never sent to the principal's office again.

Throughout the rest of the year, Michael continued to have trouble. However, no incident was as serious as the time he was accused of taking two fifty dollar bills from Mrs. Frank's purse. Mrs. Frank,

Michael's seventh grade teacher, insisted she saw him take the money.

The school board was considering expelling Michael from school for the remainder of the year. Rumor had it that Mrs. Frank was even considering notifying the sheriff's office about the theft. As the expulsion was debated among the members of the school administration, Judge Tillman paid a visit to the Tillman Farm and Tractor Company where Mrs. Frank's husband, Paul, was employed.

Instead of the crazed persona he displayed to Principal Moore, the Judge calmly approached Paul Frank, politely shaking his hand before proceeding.

"Paul," the Judge began. "Do you like your job here?"

"Of course," Paul replied without hesitation.

"Good, good." The Judge paused before continuing, hoping to emphasize his main point even more. "I would hate for something to happen that would cause you to lose it."

Surprised at how forward the Judge had suddenly become, Paul looked into his eyes and noticed a sternness he had never seen before. Of course Paul had heard about Michael's theft, everyone had. But Paul never would have expected to be confronted by the Judge about the situation.

Before he could respond, the Judge continued, "Also, I feel I should remind you that the Tillman Bank holds the mortgage on your house, and if you were to miss a payment, the Bank would be obligated to call in the whole note. I hope we understand each other, Paul." He spoke as if it was the most reasonable thing in the world.

"I…I don't know…" Paul stammered, still in shock from the Judge's bold statements. Before he was able to respond, the Judge spun on his heels and walked back through the door as quickly as he had come in.

It wasn't until later that Paul found a plain envelope on his desk containing two fifty dollar bills – a meager sum considering Judge

Tillman's affluence. With the debt paid and his threat clearly presented, Judge Tillman was confident that the matter was resolved.

The next day, Mrs. Frank revealed to the school leaders that she had misplaced the money and accidentally put it in her Christmas savings box. She insisted that it had been her fault all along.

The incident was never brought up again.

The next day, the Judge sat with his wife, Emily, in the drawing room of the Tillman estate. Emily silently flipped through a magazine as the Judge reviewed several of the Enterprise's latest financial documents.

Although the husband and wife were often seen together, they seldom spoke to each other about important issues. Devoting his life to the cause of his business conglomerate, the Judge saw little place for his wife in the world of finances and cut-throat competition. It was for this reason that the Judge was startled to hear Emily clear her throat and speak up from across the room.

"Darling," she whispered. "I think we need to talk."

The Judge raised his eyebrows and set his paperwork aside, inviting her to go on.

"I'm worried about Michael," she continued. "His behavior recently has concerned me quite a bit. He seems so upset all the time, and he was almost kicked out of school. I just don't know what to do with him. We never had this problem with his father."

The Judge shrugged and stood to his feet, pacing around the room as he considered his wife's words. He couldn't deny that the same concerns had passed through his mind a time or two in the past couple of weeks.

"I don't see any reason to worry," he finally responded, wishing to ignore the issue altogether. "He's only a boy, mischief is to be expected…"

Emily gave him a quizzical look, obviously not buying a word of what he said. "I was speaking to Matty the other day, and she seems to think that it is a problem with his character," she continued, ignoring his dismissal of her concerns. The Judge may know how to convince clients to act a certain way, but she was certainly not willing to give up on this argument.

The Judge sighed, sensing the sincerity of her words. She rarely confronted him with specific concerns, but he knew that when she did, it was better to relent than resist her admonition.

"Alright," he finally replied. "I'll talk to him about his misbehavior. There must be a way to get through to him."

Emily smiled and returned to her magazine, content that her husband would keep to his word.

Later in the day, when Michael returned from school, the Judge summoned his grandson to his office. Michael immediately knew what this was about. He knew a meeting with his grandfather was inevitable after the Judge had somehow kept him from being expelled.

Stepping into the office, Michael presented a look of sorrow and regret on his young face – an expression he had used a time or two before. However, unbeknownst to the Judge, Michael sat before the older man with complete confidence.

By now, he knew exactly how to handle the Judge.

"Papa, I am so sorry I've been such a disappointment to you over the last few years," Michael cried, before the Judge could say anything. "I have been nothing but a burden to you and Grandma ever since I got here."

He had this down to a science, and this was definitely one of his best performances yet. He even managed to eke out a tear or two.

"Please, please forgive me," the boy wailed, throwing his arms around his grandfather's waist.

Looking up into the Judge's eyes, the stern look that he had become all too familiar within the last few weeks was gone, replaced by a look of teary-eyed sorrow.

"Michael, you are no trouble to me. You are my boy and you could never be a disappointment. Now don't you worry, everything will be just fine."

He gave his grandson one last squeeze and sent him out of the room. The meeting had been much shorter than expected. As Michael closed the door to the Judge's office, his sorrowful façade was replaced with an accomplished smile. His grandfather wasn't the only skilled manipulator in the family.

Yep, he knew exactly how to handle the Judge.

Chapter 4: Refusing to Listen

"To whom can I speak and give warning? Who will listen to me? Their ears are closed so they cannot hear. The word of the LORD is offensive to them; they find no pleasure in it." Jeremiah 6:10

When Michael graduated grammar school several years later, the Judge decided that his grandson should attend a more prestigious school for the entirety of his high school education. Only a few days into his summer break, the Judge ushered him into his office to tell him about the change to be made in the fall. He expected him to be pleased with the move to Brighton Academy – one of the best private high schools in the entire state. After all, Michael had few friends at the old school.

However, as soon as he broke the news to the young boy, he could immediately sense he was unhappy about it. The Judge had forgotten an important connection to the old school that Michael would not be willing to let go: Billy.

"I can't go," Michael said bluntly. "I want to stay with Billy."

"But Michael, be reasonable," the Judge pleaded. "You'll get a much better education, and be learning with students as advanced as you are."

"No, I won't go." Michael set his jaw and refused to relent, despite the Judge's continued persuasion.

Boy, was he stubborn – just like his grandfather. The Judge couldn't help but see the irony of the situation.

He knew there was little he could do to convince him to attend Brighton, other than to somehow get Billy to attend the school as well.

"Michael, you know Billy's mother won't be able to afford Brighton. She makes hardly enough money to sustain the two of them as it is."

Michael furrowed his brow, contemplating the situation. Clearly, there was only one solution, though he didn't know how the Judge would respond.

"Either you pay for Billy to come to Brighton with me, or I won't go," Michael retorted, obviously pushing his luck. However, now that he was on a roll, he figured he might as well say more. "Also, Billy and his mom live in terrible conditions. Their house is falling apart, and you said yourself that they barely have enough money to get by. I hate to live in a house like this when the Deans have hardly anything."

This last part had been weighing on Michael's mind for a while now. He figured this was as good a time as any to bring it before the Judge.

"I know you have more than enough to help Billy and his mother a thousand times over," he continued. "If you don't at least agree to help them out a little bit, I refuse to go to Brighton in the fall." Michael could tell by the expression on the Judge's face that he hadn't expected the tables to turn on him so suddenly.

Before his grandfather could respond, Michael rose to his feet and strode out of the room, closing the door silently behind him. He knew the Judge didn't take kindly to being given an ultimatum, but he figured he had no other choice.

True, he hated the school he went to now, and the thought of going to another, more prestigious school was exciting, but he hated the thought of leaving Billy behind. He had one friend and he was not willing to jeopardize their friendship, no matter how big the opportunity.

As the summer drew to a close Michael prepared to start his first year at Brighton. The Judge had finally conceded and offered to pay the majority of Billy's tuition for the school, despite Ms. Dean's initial refusal. At first, Billy had been reluctant himself, not wanting to take advantage of the Tillman's generosity, but when the Judge insisted, they had little choice but to relent.

Judge Tillman could be a very persuasive man.

The Judge also found a way to get Ms. Dean a job at the academy, as an assistant manager in the kitchen, so that she could have a reduction in yearly tuition.

The Deans were given another surprise a week later when a group of workers sent from the Tillman Estate showed up at their door offering to refurbish their small home for free. The workers quickly began installing a new roof, vinyl siding, windows, front door, and plumbing and electrical systems, as the Deans stood by in disbelief. Within a couple of weeks, their house was already unrecognizable, completely remodeled inside and out.

Billy's mother, Janet, was overcome with gratitude for the Tillman's kindness, none of which would have been possible without Michael's agreement with the Judge.

Billy was just as excited as Michael for the year to come at Brighton Academy. Like Michael, Billy had few acquaintances at the old school and little time to enjoy extracurricular activities, since he been forced to work in order to supplement his mother's meager income.

However, with Janet's new job and much needed repairs made to their small home, Ms. Dean assured Billy that he could get involved with any clubs he wanted, without worrying about a job for the time being.

The campus reminded Billy of the Tillman property, a vast estate full of antebellum-style architecture, sweeping lawns, and intricate student centers full of numerous afterschool activities.

The first day came and went without any problems, and both boys came to love the school for all it had to offer. In the months that followed, Billy took full advantage of his newfound freedom from work, getting involved in every extracurricular activity possible.

He played sports, joined the debate team, and even joined a youth ministry on campus at the request of his mother.

The Dean family had been devout Baptists for generations, and Billy and his mother were no exception. Janet took her son to a small church every Sunday, where she played the piano and Billy sang in the choir. She was very religious and extremely concerned about her son's character, especially after seeing his growing friendship with Michael Tillman.

Michael was without a doubt the best friend Billy had ever had, and Ms. Dean was grateful for the companionship. However, she could not deny that Michael was heading down a dangerous path, due largely in part to the quality of his upbringing. She may not have given Billy the most luxurious childhood, but she undoubtedly instilled in him a sense of right and wrong.

In their first few weeks at Brighton, Janet brought her concerns before Billy, encouraging him to invite Michael to church with them the next Sunday.

Billy had tried on more than one occasion to get Michael to accompany them to church, though each time he was never given a definitive answer. He didn't know why Michael was so averse to religious organizations, but Billy swore he noticed his friend tense up every time the matter arose.

However, he figured he would appease his mother and ask one more time.

As the next Friday drew to a close, and classes let out for the weekend, Billy rushed to find Michael before heading to basketball practice.

Michael sat under a tree reading one of his history books, as Billy ran up.

"Hey," Billy exclaimed, flashing a friendly smile and sitting down next to his friend.

"Hi," Michael replied, not bothering to look up from the textbook. "Shouldn't you be at practice?"

"Yeah," Billy said, "I just wanted to ask you something first." All of a sudden he felt uncomfortable, and unsure of how to present the question. He couldn't shake the feeling that he already knew what Michael's response would be.

"What is it," Michael said, finally closing his book and putting it aside.

"Well, my mother was wondering if you would be interested in coming to church with us this Sunday. It'll only take an hour or so, and it would be a lot of fun."

He immediately noticed a change in Michael's expression. A glazed look came over his eyes and he kept looking away as if he needed to get somewhere in a hurry. "I…I don't know," Michael started to say. "I never really know what the Judge has planned for Sundays. I'll have to get back to you on that."

Here he goes again, Billy thought to himself. He had to admit that was the exact response he had expected. At least he had tried.

As Billy stood to leave, he couldn't help but push a little further. "I don't understand you Michael," he blurted out without thinking. "You are my best friend but I really don't understand you. Every time I try to be nice and invite you to church, you get closed off, and act like I insulted you. I care about you and I'm just trying to help you…"

"Help me!" Michael shouted in disbelief, standing to face Billy. "What makes you think I need your help?"

It was a rhetorical question but Billy responded anyway. "Your grandparents never take you to church and you have never once talked about God," Billy exclaimed, finally getting to the heart of his frustration. "Michael, don't you even believe in God?"

As soon as the words left Billy's mouth, Michael's face turned bright red and a tremor shot through his entire body. Billy knew he had said something wrong, he just didn't know what it was.

Michael glared at his friend for a while without responding. "Yes," he said between clenched teeth, "I believe He is a horrible, mean, and cruel God. And I hate Him."

Billy was completely taken aback by the response. He had always believed Michael to be indifferent on the subject of religion. He had never expected such abhorrence for the God that he and his mother worshipped and loved so much. "Michael…why?" It was all Billy could think to say.

Michael stared hard at the ground, tears welling up in his eyes, as he bit his lip to keep them from falling. The one subject that he had avoided for so long had finally been brought to light. He had never told Billy about the death of his parents, but he figured his friend deserved more of an explanation. "Because God took my Mama and Daddy from me when I was six years old." At this, he was no longer able to hold back the tears, and they flowed freely down his face.

"Michael, I'm so sorry. I had no idea." Billy put his arm around Michael's shoulder. "But please, you can't blame God for this."

Michael pushed Billy away, grabbed his book and turned to leave. "Don't you ever talk to me about God again Billy," he said with fire in his eyes. "I know you're just trying to help, but I do not need your help. Please just leave me alone." With that he spun on his heels and stormed off, wiping his eyes with the back of his hands.

Billy watched him as he walked away, still in shock over the unexpected exchange. Michael never ceased to surprise him, but this was a completely different story. He had never in his life met someone so opposed to God, so resistant to even merely discussing the subject of religion.

Billy's mother was right, Michael was headed down a bad path, with very few positive influences around him. Billy just hoped he hadn't alienated his best friend.

As Billy walked back toward the gymnasium, one thought refused to leave his head: Michael Tillman needed God.

Chapter 5: Different Paths

"I spread out my hands all day long to a rebellious people who walk in the wrong path, following their own thoughts." Isaiah 65:2

Their first year at Brighton Academy quickly came to an end and the boys were still the best of friends. The argument about God was a thing of the past, but it continued to weigh heavily on Billy's mind.

The boys were inseparable during the school year, but the paths they took that summer couldn't have been more different.

Billy, following his passion, got a job at Swamp Water Bait and Tackle, selling supplies and occasionally leading fishing and sightseeing trips into the Okefenokee while Michael started hanging out at the local pool hall with an older group of hoodlums who were known around town as troublemakers.

Billy worked hard and saved his money to buy a rusted out old Chevy truck and spent his free time fixing it up. It broke down on him every once in a while, but given time, he was always able to get it running again. He was proud of the old truck even if it was held together by rust.

When Michael turned sixteen that summer, his grandfather gave him a brand new, fully loaded pickup from Tillman Ford. His behavior was becoming more reckless, and his driving was the same. The local police realized soon enough that giving Michael a ticket was pointless since his grandfather would simply make a phone call and it would disappear.

When Billy wasn't working at the bait shop or fixing up his truck, he was spending time with a pretty girl he met at Church. Betty Jo, or B.J. as she was known to her friends, was the preacher's daughter, and Billy was smitten.

In stark contrast to his best friend's behavior, Michael's time was spent drinking, smoking and messing around with the trashy girls at the pool hall. He rarely thought about Billy or the times they spent together during all of the previous summers. He considered his new friends much more exciting.

As the hot summer months dragged on and Michael continued showing up at the pool hall, the gang started giving him a hard time about being a spoiled, rich brat. They said if he really wanted to fit in with them, he needed to prove himself. Late one night, they convinced him to ride along as they looked for something to vandalize. As an initiation into their group, he was told to break into a house while the owners were on vacation to steal guns, money and anything else he could carry back to the waiting car.

Michael had been in plenty of trouble in his life, but this was a whole new level of recklessness, even for him. As he busted out a back window in the house, he was shaking so badly he knocked over a lamp and tripped over the coffee table. He felt sick but wanted to prove himself to his new friends.

When he came back to the car with an armload of stolen items from the house, they all gave him high-fives and shouted out in triumph as he dumped all the pilfered goods in the trunk. Among the items were several weapons. They were secretly surprised that he went through with it but were happy to see that he was officially one of them now. In spite of their original opinion of him, he was starting to grow on them.

One Friday evening, Michael told his grandparents he was heading out to the mall and would meet up with friends for a late movie, so they shouldn't expect him home until very late. The Judge reminded Michael that he and Emily were heading out to their lake cabin for the weekend and bringing Mae Bell to help with some housekeeping since the house had been closed up for a few months. They were giving Matty the weekend off, so Michael would have to fend for himself.

The parking lot was crowded when Michael arrived at the mall, so he was forced to park in an outer lot. As he started to whip into the space, another car tried to pull in at the same time. Two men jumped out, demanding Michael move his truck while using voluminous expletives. When Michael refused to move, one of the men grabbed a stone off the ground and ran it down the side of Michael's truck, destroying the paint job.

Michael was livid as he jumped out of his truck and threw his best punch into the man's nose causing blood to pour down his face, but this was a much different fight than the schoolyard brawls he had been in before. Both men jumped on him, one held Michael's arms back while the other one beat Michael savagely almost knocking him unconscious before dumping him in the back of his truck. They drove Michael's truck to the edge of the parking lot and left him there bleeding.

With a bloody nose and swollen eye, blood dripping down his face, he managed to drive to the pool hall and told his friends what had just happened. Michael was about to find out what the gang meant when they said "mess with one of us, mess with all of us."

Four of the guys jumped in a car and followed Michael back to the mall so he could identify the other vehicle involved in the fracas. They told Michael to drive straight home, leaving the clean up to them, then they waited for the two men to return to their car.

The ambush occurred before they even realized what was happening, and by the time it was over, both men were unconscious and in a bloody heap on the pavement.

When Michael found out what they had done for him, it confirmed his belief that winners didn't play by the rules. He felt like he could get away with anything.

The next day, Michael climbed out of bed around noon feeling like he was on top of the world, knowing Matty would be happy to make him breakfast at this late hour and was preparing a story to explain all the bruises on his face.

Matty looked at him without commenting on his dreadful appearance and said, "Michael, if you come home early tonight, I'll fix a nice meal for the two of us."

"I would love to have dinner with you tonight, Matty."

Michael started walking out the door and came back, kissing her on the cheek.

"Thank you, Mat, for always being there for me and not questioning the things I do."

Matty simply said, "That's what mammas do for their babies."

When Michael returned later that day, looking forward to spending time with Matty, he discovered, to his horror, the most important person in his world lying lifeless on the kitchen floor. He ran to Matty but knew it was already too late. Doctors would later confirm that a massive heart attack took her life, but Michael knew better. God had taken his parents and now He had taken Matty, too. The loss was unbearable.

Feeling like his only lifeline to sanity had been severed, Michael waded through an emotional fog for the next few days. He hated funerals with the loss of his parents as raw and painful as the day they were laid in the ground, but he owed it to Matty to be there for her at the end.

As he stood away from the small group of mourners at the cemetery, he heard the preacher speak about God and Jesus, salvation and eternity. The crowd started singing about the Holy Spirit and souls going to heaven. His head was spinning and the pain was too great. He started crying in uncontrollable sobs and ran away from the cemetery. He wanted the hurt to go away and wanted to understand why everything always seemed to come back to God. Why did they seem so happy talking about Matty's life and singing about Jesus and her soul? Didn't they understand she was gone? He felt more alone than he had ever been in his life. She had been the constant for him during so many trials and now she was gone.

He needed to talk to someone but thinking of the crowd from the pool hall only made him feel empty. He knew Billy was the only person he could turn to for help.

Billy was devastated to hear about the death of Matty. She had been like a second mother to him during all of those visits to the Tillman Farm, but what saddened him the most was knowing how much her loss would affect Michael. He was now without an anchor and he needed help.

Billy had been spending his day off with B.J., but when he heard Michael wanted to see him, they raced to be by his side. The many weeks apart quickly faded away and seeing each other again was like old times. Michael broke down to the only person left who he trusted but was disappointed to see that he brought a girl along with him.

In spite of the awkwardness of sharing his feelings in front of B.J., Michael opened up to Billy about his anger and despair over losing Matty and about the emptiness he felt inside. Billy knew he was treading into dangerous territory with Michael but he wasn't about to give up on him even if it meant he might drive him away for good.

"Michael, you and I have been best friends for a long time, and I love you like a brother. This may be hard to hear, but I think your biggest problem is that you don't have love in your heart for anyone but yourself."

Michael couldn't believe what he was hearing as his best friend continued, "I know you cared about Matty, but I don't think you have any idea of what love really is. It's about giving of yourself, your time, your energy. When all you do is take with no concern for anyone else, you're going to feel empty inside."

He was on a roll now and even the pain on Michael's face couldn't stop him. "You surround yourself with those deadbeats at the bar who only care about having a good time, and you're just like them...but you don't have to be.

Billy continued, "Michael, you're living a sinful life, and that's why you don't want to talk about God, why you don't want to know him and why you can't love him. God is reaching out to you right now with his love calling you to himself."

"Michael, I know Matty loved you and wanted more for you than that. She was a great woman, and I miss her, too. But the pain you're feeling is for yourself. We will always miss her, but Matty is in heaven with God, our Father. That should start to give you some peace."

"Father?!" Michael yelled with distain. "Don't ever say 'Our Father!'. He is certainly not my father! I don't want anything to do with him! I thought I made that perfectly clear to you already".

B.J. had been sitting quietly listening to them talk, and as kindly as she could said, "Michael, He loves you more than you will ever know,"

Michael glared at her, shook his head at Billy, turned and walked away. He jumped in his shiny new truck with the gash down the side and sped away.

He hated to admit it, but he knew Billy was only trying to help. He thought of the great impression he had just made in front of Billy's girlfriend, but didn't he know better than to bring her along anyway? He missed Matty so much it hurt, and he felt guilty for taking her for granted all these years. He would have done anything to bring her back to thank her and hug her one more time.

As they watched the dust settle, Billy reached over and put an arm around B.J. who looked shocked by what had just happened. He said with a heavy heart, "Yep. That's my best friend."

Chapter 6: Paternal Ideology

"Beware lest any man spoil you through philosophy and vain deceit, after the traditions of men, after the rudiments of the world and not after Christ" Colossians 2:8

It took a few months, but the friends finally settled into a new normal. Billy agreed not to discuss religion in front of Michael who said he wouldn't act like a jerk around B.J. again. It was a workable plan.

He also agreed to stay away from the pool hall.

By their junior year at Brighton Academy, Michael had grown into a very attractive seventeen year old. At 6'2" with surfer, blonde hair and crystal blue eyes, he was a good looking kid, and he knew it. He had a strong, square jaw, broad shoulders and an engaging smile.

On the first day of class, Michael was slouching down in his chair with his feet resting on the seat in front of him, bored and missing the freedom of his summer vacation when in walked the most gorgeous girl he had ever seen.

He quickly sat up straight and cleared the chair in front of him. Jennifer Prescott stood at the door surveying the room and chose a seat on the other side of the classroom. He watched her sit down and cross her long, tan legs. She was 5'7" tall with long, black hair and blue-green eyes. He couldn't decide if she looked like royalty or a movie star, maybe both.

There was no denying her beauty, but she had such a friendly, open personality as she introduced herself to the classmates around her that she didn't act like someone who thought highly of herself.

Michael quickly caught up with her in the hall after class and asked if she wanted to join him at the ice cream shop across the street after school. She politely declined saying she needed to get home.

Not used to being rejected, Michael said with a bit of arrogance, "Look, Honey, I don't ask a girl out a second time if she tells me no". Jenny stopped walking, turned to Michael and with an attitude he hadn't seen from her before, said, "Well, isn't that good news!"

Still not giving up, he continued walking with her into Chemistry class. He was feeling lucky that they shared the next class, and he tried again with his irresistible charm.

"Well then, Honey, how would you like to be my lab partner? You'll find out I'm not just a pretty face. I'm pretty smart, too, and I can help you out."

Clearly irritated, Jenny said condescendingly, "No thanks. I'm pretty smart myself and I don't need your help. And how about you stop calling me Honey? I really don't like it".

Michael remained persistent and said with his best attempt at sincerity, "Looks like we've gotten off to a bad start here. Let's try again. My name is Michael Tillman. It's very nice to meet you. I would like to get to know you better."

She said firmly, "I know who you are, and I know all about your reputation. I was warned to stay far away from you".

"Oh really?" He wasn't surprised she had heard about him. Who in town didn't know about him and his family? But he wasn't about to give up. "So, who told you to stay away from me?" he asked with a sly grin.

As she walked across the room to choose another lab partner, Jenny looked over her shoulder and said, "My father…the new principal here. I'm sure you'll get to know him very well in no time".

On the way to his next class, Michael passed Billy in the hall, "Hey, Billy, what's up with that new girl, Jenny? Everybody keeps saying she's so nice, but I think she's got a major stick up her butt".

Billy stopped growing last year, so at 5'10", he looked up at his best friend and smiled, "Got rejected, did you?" He patted

Michael on the back and said, "Better luck next time, Buddy. I can't believe God's gift to women got shot down. Too bad. I don't think she likes you very much!"

Michael shot back, "She doesn't know me very much! Just wait. I'll have her eating out of my hands in no time."

Michael was in unchartered territory. His best efforts at flirting had failed, so it was time to move on to Plan B. He checked the sign-up sheets posted in the hall for after school activities. Jenny's name wasn't on any of the "fun" ones that he would have chosen. He scanned through the list of clubs and names and finally found hers listed under Bible Study. This definitely wouldn't have been at the top of his list. Not even top 100. But he was on a mission, so he would have followed her anywhere.

The group met on Thursday afternoons after school. Michael counted down the days and played it cool with Jenny in class until then. When he walked into the room for the first meeting, he found Jenny and

Billy sitting together talking about the Bible. He always knew Billy was a good wing-man, and it looked like he was already helping his buddy out.

He sat next to Billy, looked over at Jenny and winked, "Hi, Honey. Nice to see you again. Missed me?" He wasn't sure, but it looked like Jenny and Billy both cringed.

The group started discussing their personal relationships with Jesus, and Michael felt completely out of place. This wasn't helping him get any closer to Jenny. He leaned over to Billy and said, "You've been talking about God and Jesus for years. I don't know who Jesus is, but he sure doesn't want to have a relationship with any of us. This is ridiculous."

Jenny heard this and suddenly felt sorry for Michael. What kind of example of God's love was she showing him by being so dismissive? Jenny smiled at Michael and asked if he was serious about what he said.

"Honey, I don't know who God is let alone Jesus, and I really don't care to know either one of them."

"If you don't know God or follow the word of Jesus, what is your moral compass? How do you know right from wrong? Don't you know that God gave us the Holy Spirit to give us discernment to make the right choices in our lives?"

He didn't care much for the topic, but at least they were talking. "I've never bothered with the idea of morality, really. I only care about legal or illegal. And if I do something illegal, I sure as hell don't want to get caught. My grandfather told me if I wanted to be successful, I had to be better and smarter than everybody else. He says there's nothing more important than success and it doesn't matter how you get there. Wealth, power, fame…that's what's important. That buys you respect."

"That may be the worst advice I've ever heard", she said sharply. So much for feeling sorry for this guy, she thought. How could anyone be so arrogant and misguided? She tried to be sympathetic, but he was impossible.

She glared at Michael and said, "You remember this 'hot shot', you are headed for big trouble with that philosophy of yours."

"My grandfather said if I wanted something I should go after it and not let anything or anybody stand in the way."

Jennifer was horrified, "Oh, please spare me the paternal ideology."

She couldn't believe this guy. She waved him off dismissively and continued, "I can't believe I actually thought I saw something good in you! Boy, was I wrong!" With eyes blazing, she stared up at him and said, "You are an obnoxious, disagreeable, offensive, pompous jerk!"

He grinned at her and said teasingly, "Has anyone ever told you how cute you are when you're mad?"

The heat rose in her face as she snapped back, "You absolutely disgust me!"

With a hardness in his eyes, he replied, "If I want something, I go after it. If anyone gets in my way,

I'll roll over them. It would do you good to remember that, Girlie."

Everyone in the group had been watching the exchange between the two of them and hoped the conversation, if you could call it that, was over.

Michael, unable to let it go, continued as he walked toward the door, "Haven't you heard the saying 'The one with the most toys at the end wins'?"

She truly couldn't help but feel sorry for him. How could he have such an empty, meaningless life and not even realize it? Not to be outdone, she spoke up, "Yes, Michael, but haven't you heard the saying 'What will it profit a man if he gains the whole world and forfeits his immortal soul'?"

As Michael walked out the door, the entire classroom erupted in cheers and clapping in appreciation for Jenny finally putting Michael in his place. No one had ever done that before.

Chapter 7: Loneliness

"I lie awake; I am like a lonely sparrow on the housetop." Psalm 102:7

Things hadn't worked out as Michael had hoped, and he finally gave up on the idea of getting Jenny's attention. He had never had to work that hard for a girl before and he wasn't going to waste any more time on this one.

With Billy torn between studying, sports, work and his girl friend, he and Michael didn't see much of each other. He promised Billy he would stay away from the hoodlums at the pool hall, but he started to miss the companionship. He knew they weren't a great crowd, but it was better than being alone.

The old gang seemed to be happy he was back, and it didn't take long for him to feel like he belonged. If drinking, drugs and burglary were a part of the lifestyle, then so be it.

A few months after he reconnected with them, two of the guys were caught breaking into an electronics store. They were repeat offenders carrying stolen weapons in the commission of a crime, and it didn't look good for them. Their attorneys worked out a plea bargain. They would get a lighter sentence if they said where they got the guns. Blaming Michael was easy and no one doubted their story.

The police arrived at Brighton Academy and arrested Michael in front of his classmates, but his grandfather had him out of jail within a few hours. Without any proof, the District Attorney couldn't make the charges stick, but the damage was done. Michael was finished with the gang at the pool hall for turning him in and the students at Brighton stayed as far away from him as possible. No one wanted to be associated with him.

He finished up the school year feeling more alone than ever before. Summers were supposed to be spent with friends. He know everyone would be out swimming, boating and waterskiing on the lake and spending time together at parties and dances, but Michael wasn't included. They would all be talking about college plans after their last year in high school, and he didn't know what he was going to do. College seemed so far off and not something he really wanted to do anyway. He just knew he was so very alone.

As he was laying on his bed one evening, the Judge came in and sat next to him.

"Michael, you and I need to talk. We've got to start making some serious plans about your future."

Michael threw a pillow over his face and groaned, "I'm not in the mood to talk. Especially not about anything serious. Please leave me alone."

He could tell his grandfather was getting angry. "Well, you'd better get in the mood. And you will listen to what I have to say. Do you understand?"

He reluctantly agreed as his grandfather continued, "You'll be eighteen soon and going into your senior year. Have you given any thought about where you want to go to college after graduation? What you might want to study?"

Michael leaned up on his elbow and said, "Papa, I don't even think I want to go to college. I've been thinking I'd really like to travel around the country. Maybe to Europe. See new places."

"Michael, your grandmother and I are getting older. I'm not sure how much more time I have left. While I'm still able, I want to teach you about the family business. You are the rightful heir, but you've got to be more responsible. I can't trust something this important to someone who lies around all day and has no ambition. And all that trouble with the police? You have to be prepared. Your father was prepared, and you owe it to him."

Michael jumped off the bed and shouted, "Like hell! I don't owe him a damn thing! He left me alone. They all left me. I didn't have anyone who cared about me, except for Matty. Someone once told me that I didn't know how to love. I feel like there's no love inside me. Hell, no wonder. Matty was the only person who really cared about me!"

Michael was trying to speak between sobs. There were many times he used tears to manipulate his grandfather, but this was not a ploy; this was real.

"Michael, I am so sorry. You have to believe I've tried, but I know I've never been able to help you, to fill the void you feel from losing your parents. Your grandmother and I were broken hearted, too. We just thought we could fill the emptiness by giving you things. That you'd be happy with us because of all we could provide for you. I'm sorry it wasn't enough."

He had never seen his grandfather cry, to drop his guard and be vulnerable and for the first time in his life, he actually felt sorry for the Judge.

He hugged Michael and said, "I don't know who can help you, but I do know that you can't run away from your problems. Your demons will follow you wherever you go, will be with you in every relationship and will destroy all of your life experiences. I don't want that kind of future for you. I'll do whatever I can to help you. I just wish I knew what that was." He turned away with his head down and left Michael alone again in his room.

The next morning, Michael knocked on his grandfather's office door, walked in and sat down. He said he was ready to learn about the business. They shook hands, the emotions of the previous night far behind them, and spent the next few hours together discussing Michael's birthright.

The Judge told Michael that the family had a great responsibility to the thousands of people whose livelihoods depended on their success.

He explained how the farm and the Tillman Enterprise were a conglomerate made up of a large number of companies in many different fields: real estate, commercial businesses, banking, manufacturing, forestry, agriculture, and rail roads with a value of over $2 billion.

"Michael, it may seem overwhelming, but I built this myself. I've surrounded myself with the best advisors who will someday be there for you. This is your responsibility, but you will never be in it alone. I have lawyers, bankers, accountants who are like family. You will be able to trust them like I have. If you study hard, take courses in management and finance, in a few years of working with me, you'll be ready to handle it yourself. Promise me you'll take this seriously."

"I will, Judge, I promise", Michael said, as he secretly wondered how he could ever do it.

Jenny ran into Billy and B.J. at a picnic over the summer. She was still irritated by Michael's arrogant behavior, but something about his bitterness and anger toward God had stayed with her. She sat down on their blanket and asked Billy about it. He hadn't told anyone other than B.J. about

Michael's history, but something about Jenny's concern compelled him to share with her. He told the story of the accident that took his parents away when he was six and how Michael always blamed God. He told her about the grandparents who tried their best giving Michael everything but direction. He shared with her all of the things that made Michael the irritating best friend that he was, but he was surprised by her questions. "I thought you didn't like him. Why the sudden interest?"

"He said he hated God, yet he had no idea what it meant to have a personal relationship with Jesus. That has really been bothering me, and I'm worried about his salvation. I think he likes me, or used to, and if I can use that connection to talk to him about God and explain things to him, I have to try. I've been praying about it. Believe me. This is the last thing that I would normally want to do!"

After the first day of school, it was such beautiful weather that Michael stopped off at the stadium to soak in the sun before heading home. Everyone seemed happy to be back, and there were other kids sitting on the bleachers and walking around the track while the football team practiced in the field. Michael sat on the end of the bleachers away from the other students and stared into space. After a few minutes, he felt someone standing near him, and he turned around to see the last person on earth he would have expected.

With a smile, Jenny asked if she could sit with him.

Michael said, "Yes, please have a seat, Honey." But this time it was said as an inside joke instead of condescendingly as he had in the past.

Jenny smiled back at him and said, "I thought I told you not to call me honey."

They sat quietly for a few minutes, then Jenny said, "I haven't seen you around much lately. Is everything okay?"

"Sure, yep. Just great. I'm cool" he said trying to cover the heaviness he was feeling.

Knowing it was time for tough love, she replied, "No, Michael. You are not cool. You are an undisciplined, conceited, spoiled brat." Before Michael could say anything, she continued, "Billy also told me about your mom and dad. Michael, you are so wrong about God. He really does love you."

"Yeah, I think you told me that once before."

"You remembered", she said pretending surprise. "Michael, if you'll let me, I know I can help you. This is our senior year. We will all be graduating soon and heading off in different directions.

"I'm going to UGA and want to study accounting so I can be a CPA. What are your plans?"

"My grandfather wants me to go there, too, but I'm not sure that college is really for me."

"Oh, Michael! That would be wonderful. We would be there together", she quickly stopped herself and stammered, "I don't mean 'together'. I didn't mean it that way. I meant, we will be there, you know, at the same time, not together."

He grinned at her momentary discomfort.

"Michael, if you let me help you, I promise I will never quit on you". She could see that her words were making an impact on him. "I want to be your friend, and I will always be there for you. I will never leave you. She paused and continued, "Will you do me a favor?"

"You know I will do anything for you, Jen."

"Please take this Bible and read John 1 verses 1-5. Read it over and over as many times as you can. Then read the rest of the chapter. We can meet back here in a couple of days."

"What about tomorrow?"

"It's a lot of reading. I think you'll need some time to get through it."

"Hey, I'm a fast reader." He skimmed through the pages she pointed out to him as he continued, "Yep, no problem."

"Okay, great then. I'll see you tomorrow."

As she walked down the stairs, Michael called out in a loud voice, "Bye, Honey!"

She continued walking, smiling to herself, and without turning around, she waved one arm in the air and replied loudly, "I told you, don't call me that!"

As she drove off, she thought about everything Billy told her of Michael's childhood. Growing up in such a loving home, she couldn't begin to imagine how he felt after losing his parents. She could see the pain in his eyes behind his confident façade, and she desperately wanted to help him understand the hope that comes from the Lord. She wanted to reach him and help him know that, in spite of everything, God loves him and wants him in heaven for all eternity. Baby steps. At least they were talking.

When Michael got home, he jumped out of his truck and took the front steps two at a time. He ran into the Judge's office where he was sitting at his desk.

"Papa, I've thought more about what you said, about college. I've decided I want to go to UGA. Maybe study accounting."

The Judge was shocked at this new level of enthusiasm. He stood up and gave him a big hug, "I am so proud of you, Michael."

"I'm going to study hard, and I'll be ready when the time comes."

With a new bounce to his step, Michael turned and walked out of the room. The Judge called after him, "What's that book you've got there."

Michael looked down at the Bible in his hand and replied, "Oh, nothing. Just a book."

Chapter 8: Hearing the Word-Baptism

"So faith comes from hearing, and hearing through the word of Christ." Romans 10:17

"We were buried therefore with him by baptism into death, in order that, just as Christ was raised from the dead by the glory of the one Father we too might walk in newness of life." Romans 6:4

Michael went up to his room, threw the Bible on his desk and lit a joint, thinking how great it would be if he and Jen spent the next four years together at college. He took a nap and when he awoke, he stared at the ceiling playing their conversation over in his head, but his eyes kept drifting back to his desk and the Bible. He decided he better read through it so he could talk to Jen about it the next day.

When he opened the Bible to the book of John, the first words he read were "The Word became flesh". He read over it a few times, trying to understand the meaning and decided to give up and continue reading. In verses 1-5 he read, "In the beginning was the Word, and the Word was with God, and the Word was God. All things were made through Him and without Him was not anything made that was made. In Him was life and the life was the light of men. The light shines in the darkness and the darkness has not overcome it."

Michael read each line over and over but wasn't able to figure out what any of it meant.

The next day, Michael arrived at the stadium to find Jennifer sitting in their same place. When he sat down, she asked, "So, did you finish reading everything we talked about yesterday?"

"Are you kidding me? I never got past the first few sentences! I'm a pretty smart guy. I can usually read something and figure it out, but this didn't make sense to me at all. 'The Word was with God. The Word was God. The Word was life and light and whatever' Sounds like some kind of riddle."

"No, Michael, its not a riddle", she grinned. "Let me try to explain. God is our Creator. Our Father. And he is a spirit."

"Okay. I think I heard that when I was a kid. Something about God being a spirit."

"Yes. Now in the spirit there are three persons, God the Father, God the Son and God the Holy Spirit."

"So…like three little Gods under the main God?"

"Well, not exactly. Its three equal Gods that make up one God we call the Godhead. Three persons in the one spirit, the Godhead. The three persons bring about our salvation. Are you with me?"

He wasn't but he said, "Sure, go on."

Jennifer continued, "God the Father created us, God the Son died on the cross to atone for our sins, and the Holy Spirit gives us life. He guides us, councils us and lives in us."

Michael shook his head, "Wait! Wait! You've lost me. Something about atoning for our sins, salvation and something living in us doesn't make any sense."

"Michael, this is an awful lot to take in at one time. Why don't you read a little more, and it will hopefully start making more sense to you. We can talk again tomorrow. Oh, by the way, were you ever baptized?"

"Uh, I'm not really sure what that is."

"People who believe are baptized in Christ, who died for our sins and was raised from the dead. I believe in one baptism of all believers into one body which is the result of the regenerating work of the Holy Spirit when one becomes a genuine believer in Christ. There is a profound spiritual unity of all genuine believers who are 'in Christ' founded on 'one faith' in 'one Lord' irrespective of denominational differences."

Jen continued, "Holy Baptism is the basis of the whole Christian life, the gateway to life in the Spirit. Through baptism, we are freed from sin and reborn as sons and daughters of God. We become members of Christ. We are incorporated into the Church and made sharers in his mission.

"Michael, you can find references to Baptism in the Bible in Acts 2:38-39: 'And Peter said to them, repent and be baptized, every one of you in the name of Jesus Christ for the forgiveness of your sins, and you will receive the gift of the Holy Spirit. For the promise is for you and for your children and for all who are far off, everyone whom our Lord our God calls to himself.'"

Michael gave a short laugh and said, "Jen, are you kidding me? You can't possibly believe that."

"It is a lot to grasp at one time, but I promise, you'll understand. And when you do, your life will change forever."

Michael got up and said, "I'll walk you to your car."

As she got in, he smiled and said, "See you tomorrow, Honey". Then he added, "Sorry, I know you don't like for me to call you that."

She looked up at him and said with a smile, "Its okay. I kind of like it." As she drove off, and

Michael stood in the parking lot shaking his head and thinking: I'll never figure that girl out!

As soon as he got home, he asked his grandmother if he had ever been baptized. She answered, "Good heavens, child. I have no idea. I'll call your Aunt Catherine to see if she knows."

Michael hurried up to his room, and his grandmother went in search of the Judge asking him, "What in the world has gotten into that boy? He's running around like a crazy person."

The Judge grinned, "I don't know, but I think he's in love."

Michael sat down and immediately started reading. This time in John 3:3-7 he read: 'Jesus declared, I tell you the truth, no one can see the kingdom of God unless he is born again. How can a man be born when he is old, Nicodemus asked. Surely he cannot enter a second time into his mother's womb to be born. Jesus answered, I tell you the truth, no one can enter the kingdom of God unless he is born of water and the

Spirit. Flesh gives birth to flesh but the Spirit gives birth to spirit. You should not be surprised at my saying. You must be born again.'

He read on in verses 16-22: For God so loved the world, that he gave his only Son, that whoever believes in him should not perish but have eternal life. For God did not send his Son into the world to condemn the world but in order that the world might be saved through Him. Whoever believes in him is not condemned, but whoever does not believe is condemned already because he did not believe in the name of the only Son of God. And this is the judgment, the light has come into the world and the people loved the darkness rather than the light because their works were evil. For everyone who does wicked things hates the light and does not come into the light, lest his works be exposed. But whoever does what is true comes to the light so that it may be clearly seen that his works have been carried out in God.

Michael read these passages over and over again until he was sure he knew what they meant. He thought of Jennifer and hoped she would be impressed with him and he fell asleep.

The next day, they met again, and Jennifer could see the excitement in Michael's face as he ran up the stadium steps. He said, "Good news. My aunt said I was baptized as a baby and my family was Escapelian."

Jennifer laughed, "I think you mean… Episcopalian? That's great."

"Jen, I think I understand what it means to be born again. It means we were born in the flesh but when we accept Jesus and get baptized, we are born again in the spirit. So cool, I'm a spirit."

Jennifer leaned over to give him a hug and kissed him on the cheek. "That's wonderful, Michael. Now, there are a few more things I want you to understand. You see, God created man in His image for His glory, which means that man is like God and represents God on earth. While everything in creation, to some degree, reflects something of who God is, humans alone are made in the image and likeness of God. When I say we are like God, we are not God nor will we ever be. God is the source of all human value. The fall of man and the curse of humanity distorts the image of God in man but does not remove it from him."

"What fall of man," Michael asked.

"We'll talk about that another time, but for now let's stay with creation for a little longer. God is infinitely perfect and created man in His image. He didn't do that because he needed us or because he was lonely. He loved us and wanted us to share in Him and His creation. It was part of His eternal plan. He wants us to seek Him, to know Him, to love Him with all our hearts, our souls, our minds and our strengths. He calls together all people, all sinners, in the unity of His family, the Church. God sent His son as a redeemer and savior as a sacrifice for our sin so we can be with Him. The Holy Spirit is the third person of the Trinity. He is equal to the

Father and Son but different in his role and relationship. The roles have the Father willing, the Son accomplishing and the Holy Spirit applying the work of the Son. The Holy Spirit is here with us, living in us. I know this is kind of confusing, but I hope it is starting to make sense."

"Well….yes, a little, but I have a million questions"

Jen smiled and said, "That's more than you had a few days ago."

Michael hesitated and said, "Jen, tomorrow is Saturday. Maybe we can do something."

"Like what."

"Have you ever been horseback riding?"

"No. I've never been on a horse before. They make me kind of nervous."

"We have a really gentle quarter horse named Belle that you can ride. It's just like sitting in a rocking chair. I'll make a picnic lunch."

"You mean you'll get your housekeeper to make lunch!"

"No. Really! I'll fix something. Whatever you like."

Jennifer said, "Ok. Surprise me. It sounds like fun."

"Okay. I'll pick you up at 10:30 tomorrow morning. What do you think your father will say?"

With a grin Jen said, "I guess he'll say 'Hello, Michael. Remember...no funny business!'"

"Hahaha. I promise I'll let him know I'll be a perfect gentleman."

Chapter 9: Sharing

"Do not neglect to do good and to share what you have, for such sacrifices are pleasing to God." Hebrews 13:16

The next morning, Michael arrived at the Prescott home right on time and hoped her father, the school principal, wouldn't be the one answering the door. Michael wasn't sure how he would be received with such a bad reputation around school. As luck would have it, Tom Prescott answered the door and greeted him coolly, "Michael, come in. Jenny will be down soon."

Michael said nervously, "Thank you, Mr. Prescott. How are you, Sir?"

"Fine." He wasn't about to engage this boy in an in-depth conversation, but he would be respectful for his daughter's sake.

Michael shifted his weight from one foot to another and said it looked like it was going to be a nice day.

"Yes it does."

Michael asked, "How is Mrs. Prescott?"

"Fine."

Jennifer came running down the stairs, saving him from more uncomfortable conversation. She looked like a cowgirl in her blue jeans, checkered shirt, western hat and boots.

"Hi, Michael. Sorry I'm late. Bye Daddy."

She kissed her father on the cheek.

Mr. Prescott said, "Have a good time, Jenny, and be safe. Goodbye Michael. Be careful."

The drive out to the stable was comfortable as they joked with each other, and Michael commented, "How do you always cleverly outwit me?"

"That's easy. I'm just smarter than you."

Michael grinned and replied, "Sure. That'll be the day."

Nothing was said for a few minutes when Michael finally said, "Do you really think so?"

Jennifer started laughing and said, "Don't tell me I've bruised your fragile male ego."

As they turned onto Tillman Farm Road, Jennifer was stunned by the beauty, "Wow! This looks like a primeval forest. I can't believe how gorgeous it is out here."

Michael gave his best scary voice, "You should see it in the pitch black darkness of the night, when you hear the coyotes calling to each other, the frogs and owls making crazy noises and the shadows from the moss hanging down from the trees like skeleton hands. It's real spooky. When I was a little boy, my um, Matty, told me about the wampus that lived in the forest but only came out at night."

"A wampus? What in the world is that," Jennifer asked.

"I don't know, and I don't want to know, but I sure don't walk around in there at night."

The forest opened up to a beautiful green pasture surrounded by four board fences running 200 yards past the grand house with the stable in the distance.

Jen gasped, "Michael, oh my gosh! This is the most beautiful house I have ever seen!" There were magnificent columns and massive stairs leading to two huge oak front doors. A covered porch ran along the front and sides of the home.

"Michael, you live here? I can't believe this place. The stable is bigger than three houses put together." He was so accustomed to it that he often forgot the awe it inspired when someone saw it for the first time. They walked over to the fence as several of the horses ran up to greet them.

Michael rubbed the nose of a large bay mare as Jennifer asked uneasily, "Will they bite?"

Replying with a grin he said, "Only if you bite them first!"

"Are we going to ride these horses? They are really big!"

"No, not these girls. The ones in this pasture are my Grandad's thoroughbreds that he raises as a hobby. These are a few of his best brood mares. When the foals are about a year old, he sells them to people who train them for racing or maybe hunter jumpers.

He grabbed her hand and headed toward the barn, "Let me introduce you to Belle."

Nate, the barn manager, had the horses saddled and ready to go when they arrived. Michael showed Jennifer how to get on the horse, how to keep her heels down in the stirrups and how to hold the reins. He walked Belle around for a few minutes until Jennifer felt more comfortable.

"Jen, You'll enjoy Belle. She's yours to ride any time you want. She's a gentle old girl, and you'll feel like you're sitting in a rocking chair."

Michael took the picnic basket and blanket and tied them to the back of his saddle on his dappled gray Quarter Horse, Tex, and they headed out to the trail head that would take them throughout the estate. Michael asked Jen several times if she wanted to stop for lunch, but she was enjoying it so much she didn't want it to end.

They continued on for another hour until they came upon one of his favorite spots. The private lake on the Tillman estate had large boulders on one side where he and Billy spent many summer hours fishing and talking.

Jen said, "This is a perfect spot. I love it!"

They climbed up on the rocks and talked. Michael told Jen about the Indians who used to live in that part of Georgia hundreds of years ago.

"My dad came here and explored these rocks when he was a boy. He used to find arrow heads of all different sizes. He put them in a display case that's still hanging in the library at the house. He also found an old canoe that had been dug out with crude tools. I've found a few things over the years, but not as much as my dad."

They sat quietly for a few minutes while Jen gave Michael space to think.

He finally said, "In all our talks about the Bible, I don't think you've ever mentioned happiness. Isn't it important?"

"Yes. It is important. People are always looking for happiness, but what's more important than happiness is contentment. That doesn't change with the wind because of your circumstances. And I also think that we were put on this earth, not for success, but for significance. Life isn't about acquiring wealth or material things or gaining fame or power. None of those worldly things will ever bring you real happiness. I think it comes from accomplishing something meaningful and significant……giving back and helping others."

Michael thought about this and asked, "I wonder why the Bible doesn't say much about happiness?"

Jen thought for a second. "Well, Jesus did talk about it in several indirect ways. In the Sermon on the Mount in Matthew 5 you can read about the Beatitudes where Jesus uses the term "blessed". It is more than a temporary feeling of happiness. It's a state of well-being.

The horses started walking away in search of better grass, so Michael helped Jen down off the rocks to secure them better.

They spread the blanket and set up the picnic under a large oak tree. When Michael pulled out the sandwiches, Jen said, "How did you know tuna fish was my favorite?"

He also pulled out deviled eggs that his grandmother helped him make, a thermos filled with lemonade, and brownies and fruit for dessert. Jen grinned at him, obviously pleased with the thought he put into their day.

"So your grandfather raises Thoroughbreds for fun. What else goes on here at the farm?"

"It's kind of complicated. When we talk about "the farm" it's not just the land here that's about 10,000 acres around the house and barns. It also includes 40,000 acres off Baldwin Road, and at last count, about 200,000 acres scattered around South Georgia and North Florida. Most of its planted in pine trees. That's what my grandfather enjoys the most, his lumber yard and saw mills.

"He also has a hunting and fishing preserve with about half a dozen luxury cabins where people can stay for a couple of thousand dollars a pop depending on what they're hunting for and how long they stay. There's a pretty cool club house with a bar, dining area and a huge fireplace. I'll have to take you there sometime. The guy who cooks for my granddad is well known around here. I think you'd really like it. He doesn't just cook wild game. I'm sure he'd be happy to make you a tuna sandwich!"

Jen smiled and waited for him to continue.

"There's also a meat processing facility, but that would probably gross you out. The guests bring their game back to the facility where it's packaged and frozen for them to take when they leave. People come there to hunt and fish from all over the country and even from overseas. My dad learned to hunt there when he was little, back when granddad had more time."

Michael continued, "Of course you saw the horses. The caretaker of all the livestock is Goose Gobbler. I seriously doubt that's his real name. Anyway, everybody just calls him Goosie. He's in charge of about 50 horses, anywhere from 25-50 hunting dogs, around 3,000 head of cattle, and the wild turkey, quail, and deer program. My Granddad keeps a full time veterinarian on staff and two mechanics to look after all the farm equipment. He mainly grows cotton on about 10,000 acres each year but I think he's grown peanuts and tobacco over the years, too. It takes a lot of people to keep it running, but somehow Papa keeps it going. And that doesn't even include all his other business. He wants me to learn all about it, but I'm afraid I don't have his natural talent."

"Wow. I had no idea he was involved in so much stuff. No wonder everybody in town seems to know your name. The Tillmans must own all of South Georgia."

Michael looked down at the crumbs from his sandwich and

replied, "Not yet, but he's working
on it."

Chapter 10: Love-Faith-Predestination

"Beloved, let us love one another, for love is from God, and whoever loves has been born of God and knows God." 1 John 4:7

"God predestined us for adoption as sons through Jesus Christ, according to the purpose of his will." Ephesians 1:5

"Therefore since we have been justified by Faith, we have peace with God through our Lord Jesus Christ." Romans 5:1

They sat on the picnic blanket under the shadowing oak until the sun started to set. Jen told Michael about her idyllic childhood growing up in Tallahassee with her two older brothers, Jim now in medical school in Augusta, and Harry who just started a job in Atlanta, and her twin brothers, John and Noah, who recently turned 13. Being the middle child and the only girl made for an interesting if not sometimes chaotic childhood, but the way she described her family and the obvious love and affection they had for each other, stirred a deep sadness and regret for the loneliness and isolation that was so pervasive in his life. He missed his parents and the time he would never get back. And he missed Matty.

Jen, aware of the change in Michael's demeanor, decided to take the opportunity to steer their conversation back to a spiritual discussion.

"You know, Michael, as a Christian, I firmly believe that Jesus died for my sins. It's pretty awesome to think that He sees me as worthy of saving, just as you are worthy. Christ rose from the dead and is our living Savior. If we believe, someday we will be raised up to spend eternity in Heaven with Him. That means that death is no longer a terrifying thing. As it says in 1 Corinthians 15:55: 'Oh death, where is your victory? Oh death, where is your sting?' I know that's a hard thing to understand, especially with all the loss you've suffered, but there really is so much more."

Michael watched the horses as they stood half sleeping in the shade and didn't reply.

Not wanting to lose this opportunity to share with him, she continued, "You may have heard the famous verse, John 3:16, that say: 'For God so loved the world that He gave his only son that whoever believes in Him shall not perish but have everlasting live.'"

"I've seen the signs at baseball games, but I never knew what it meant. I just don't understand why it was necessary for Jesus to die for us."

"To explain that, you have to go back to Adam and Eve. God created the first man and woman as His children here on Earth to be in fellowship with Him, but they disobeyed Him by trusting their own ability to discern good and evil. As a result, mankind has suffered ever since. Jesus, who was totally without sin, was offered up as a sacrifice on our behalf. He died willingly on a cross to take our sin, so we could be reconciled with God. It's important to know that he died but rose from the dead three days later. Jesus said: 'I am the resurrection and the life. Whoever believes in me though he die, yet shall he live.'"

"Jen, I really want to believe what you're saying is true, but I just don't."

"I understand this is hard for you, but if you really want to believe, pray to God and ask him to help your unbelief. Do you remember telling me you didn't think you knew what love was? The Bible tells us so much about it. In Corinthians, Paul explains how uniquely important love is when he says: 'If I speak with the tongues of men and of angels but have not love, I am but a noisy gong or a clanging symbol. And if I have the gift of prophesy and understand all mysteries and all knowledge, and though I have all faith as to move mountains, but have not love, I am nothing'. The Bible goes on to define love as patient and kind; it does not envy or boast; it does not insist on its own way; it is not irritable or resentful; it does not rejoice at wrongdoing but rejoices with the truth. Love bears all things, believes all things, hopes all things, it endures all things."

"Well, Jen, if that's what love is, it's no wonder Billy said he didn't think I had any love in me. I'm all the things that love isn't."

"You may see yourself that way, but that's not how God sees you."

Jen continued, "Michael, there is something very important for you to know. In John 17:20-26, it tells of Jesus' last prayer to the Father just before he was arrested and condemned to death on the cross. He prays for unity so the world will know the Lord sent his son and he loved humanity even as he loved Jesus. He prayed for all of them to be one in Jesus just as the father and son are one."

The ride back to the barn was mostly in silence while Michael thought of all the things Jen had said to him about love and salvation as the crickets began their nightly ritual and the horses' hooves beat out a steady rhythm on the trail home.

On the drive back to her house, Jen asked Michael to join her at Church the next day. She could sense his hesitation, but not wanting to miss a chance to be with Jen, he agreed.

At school on Monday, their connection was becoming evident to all the watchful eyes of the other students. At lunch, Jen sought out Michael and sat down with him.

"What you got there, Mike?"

"Tuna sandwich."

She smiled and said, "Me, too!" As they laughed, their eyes locked for more than a few moments. They looked away quickly but not quickly enough. Everyone in the cafeteria witnessed this special moment.

Almost instinctively, Michael reached out and took Jen's hand as they walked out of the school that afternoon to sit at the stadium together. Within the hour, gossip started running rampant:

"I saw them sitting together in Church yesterday."

"I saw Michael at Jenny's house on Saturday morning."

"I saw them holding hands at school."

"Did you see them together at lunch?"

And so it went for the next week and continued on until graduation.

During the summer, they were inseparable, spending many hours together horseback riding, fishing, swimming, and they had many more picnics with countless hours together talking. Michael also continued going to Church with Jen.

After a sermon about faith one Sunday, Michael asked Jen to explain the topic to him so he could understand it better.

She expounded, "To be human, man's response to God by faith must be free and therefore nobody is forced to embrace it against his will. God calls us to serve Him in spirit and in truth, so we are bound to Him in conscience but not coerced. Jesus invites people to faith and conversion but never coerces them. Jesus bore witness to the truth but refused to use force to impose it on those who spoke against it. We must believe in Jesus Christ and the one who sent him for our salvation. Without faith, it is impossible to please God or obtain eternal life."

Michael looked at Jen and said just one word, "Amazing."

He continued to ask questions and wanted to understand what made Jen so special and content in her life. On a trip to their favorite picnic spot by the rocks, Jen shared more.

"There's a Christian doctrine that many people debate and it's hard to understand."

"So pretty much like everything else you've been talking to me about," Michael said with a grin.

"Have you ever heard the word 'predestined'?"

"Yep, sort of determined in advance?"

"Right," Jen said as she pulled a small New Testament Bible from her bag. She opened it to Ephesians 1:3 and began to share: 'God the Father of our Lord Jesus Christ, who has blessed us in Christ even as he had chosen us in Christ before the foundation of the world. In love, he has predestined us for adoption as sons and daughters through Jesus Christ, according to the purpose of His will. In Christ, we also, when we heard the word of truth, the gospel of our salvation and believed in Christ, we were sealed with the promised Holy Spirit who is the guarantee of our inheritance until we acquire possession of it, to the praise of his glory.'

Jen continued, "In Romans 8:29 it says, 'For those he foreknew he also predestined to be conformed to the image of his Son, and those he predestined, he also called and those he called, he also justified and those he justified he also glorified.'"

"In Romans 9:19, the question is why does God still find fault? 'For who can resist God's will? The answer is… who are you O man to answer back to God? If God chooses some for destruction to show his wrath and chooses others by the riches of his glory, beforehand for glory.'"

"It's a hard concept to understand that God knows all from the beginning of time and until the end, and He knows who will accept Him. We have the free will to choose, but He already knows the outcome. It is by the grace of God that by our free will we accept Christ as our Savior and Lord."

Michael thought about that for a while and answered, "You're right. It's an odd concept to grasp. But what makes the Christian religion so different from all the other world religions?"

Jen answered, "I believe it's because Christianity is not a religion. It's a relationship with Christ."

As summer came to a close, Michael and Jen took a final ride out to the lake. "Michael, before we leave this beautiful spot, I want to share something else with you that I believe more than anything in this world."

She brought out her Bible again and turned to 1 John 3:21 and read,

Beloved, if our heart condemn us not, then we have confidence before God. And whatsoever we ask, we receive of him, because we keep his commandments and do those things that are pleasing in his sight. And this is his commandment that we should believe on the name of his son Jesus Christ and love one another just as he commanded us. Whoever keeps his commandments abides in God and God in him, and by this we know he abides in us, by the spirit whom he has given us.

She explained, "If you break all that down, the passage is saying that if we are sincere in our faith, we can come to God with boldness asking for mercy and grace in our time of need. He delights in blessing the upright and humble souls, but without a renewing of our hearts, loving God or man is impossible. This renewal comes through Christ Jesus, and the proof that God is in us is the Spirit he has given us, and the effect is in our hearts and lives."

Michael hugged Jen, wishing they could freeze time at this very spot. He still had so much unresolved anger toward God, but this incredible girl wanted him to understand and feel the joy she so clearly had in her life. He wanted it too, but the walls he had built up over the years were just so high. Not wanting her to be disappointed in him, he changed the subject.

"My granddad named this area Lonesome Pine because of that huge tree standing all by itself over yonder."

Jen smiled at him and teased, "Over yonder? Really, Michael? Over yonder?"

"You know what I mean. Over there. Over in the field. Over…"

Jen smiled, "Yonder?"

"Well, however you want to say it, I think we should carve our initials in that tree to remember this summer."

Still teasing she said, "I reckon we could do that before we have to mosey on back."

They both burst out laughing as they walked hand in hand across the green field to etch the initials JP + MT into the lonesome pine.

Chapter 11: Power of Prayer

"Continue steadfastly in prayer, being
watchful in it with thanksgiving."
Colossians 4:2

In August, they both entered
the University of Georgia in
Athens and gradually saw less and
less of each other as their lives
went in different directions.
Eventually, they didn't see each
other at all.

Michael's grandmother died in
the winter of his junior year. The
Prescott family sent a beautiful
bouquet of flowers, and the entire
family attended the funeral. Jen and
her parents offered their
condolences and Jen left him with a
hug and a promise to keep him in her
prayers. Another loss in his life
and more talk of prayer. He was
happy to see Jen and appreciated the
gesture, however empty he thought it

might be. He sent a note to her parents thanking them for their kindness.

Yet, seeing her brought back memories of their time together and especially the last summer before college. Before he left for Athens, he rode Tex back out to Lonesome Pine and ran his fingers over the rough initials they carved in the bark. He decided to be a better friend and check up on her when he got back to campus.

It wasn't long before he discovered she had been dating a boy from church, and people were talking about it being serious. It didn't make any sense, but Michael was furious. He found her boyfriend coming out of class and demanded that he stay away from Jen.

The threat was clear. Stay away or there will be problems. He threatened to hit him. He wasn't sure where it came from, but he said, "You see her again and I'll punch your lights out!" He dared him to try to see her again because he was more than happy to prove he was serious. After all, he learned a long time ago that you take what you want, and he wanted this boy away from her.

When Jen heard what happened, she called Michael and asked to meet at the student center later that day. He thought that was a positive step as he walked in and saw her already sitting at a table in the corner. As he walked toward her, he could see the anger in her eyes and her lips were pressed tightly together.

When he sat down, she immediately started yelling at him, "Who do you think you are threatening a friend of mine? What makes you think you can tell me who I can date? Michael, I will see whomever I want, whenever I want, and it's none of your business! Do you understand me?"

She had been mad at him before, but he had never seen her this upset. She continued her tirade, "Michael, I'm so angry with you I could, I could" she couldn't think of what to say and the next thing out of her mouth was, "I could punch your lights out!"

Michael could hardly keep from laughing but didn't want to make things any worse. She wasn't finished. "If you are going to be so possessive of me, I don't want you in my life. Please stay away from me and stay away from my friends."

She got up and started to walk away but turned and said more calmly, "Michael, it was sweet of you to send my folks a thank you note. They appreciated it."

Then she stormed out of the student center while Michael sat stunned and thought to himself, "I will never understand that girl."

Early in their senior year, Michael started a relationship with a girl in Jen's building with a reputation that was questionable at best and more often described as depraved. When Jen heard details about it from some of their mutual friends, she was shocked. She would often see his truck parked in front of her apartment for days at a time, and one day, they ran into each other in the parking lot. Seeing Michael there, she went into a rage and was so mad she could hardly breathe. She ran up to Michael and started screaming.

"Damn you, Michael! Damn you! How could you do this to me? How could you care so little about me and hurt me like this!"
As she screamed, tears were streaming down her face. Everyone in the parking lot turned to see what was happening.

Michael, in complete shock said, "What the hell's wrong with you? Stop! I don't know what you're talking about! What are you screaming about?"

"I've seen your truck here, so don't try to deny it! You've been practically living here with, with . . . that girl. Do you love her?"

"Jen, of course not. I don't care about her at all."

"Don't you see, that makes it even worse?" Jen was still crying, tears running down her face, as Michael stared at her in disbelief.

"Michael, why didn't you just kill me? Why did you have to rip my heart out? And you didn't just hurt me. You're hurting yourself. Do you not remember any of the things we talked about? About living a life pleasing to God and not just for yourself?"

Jen took a deep breath and continued quietly, "Do you know why I stayed away from you all this time? Why I didn't keep dating you in college? It wasn't because I didn't want to be with you, it was because I cared for you, too much. I was 18 years old with four years of college ahead of me. Michael, I fell in love with you, and I wasn't ready for that. I wanted to finish college first, then when we went back home, maybe . . ."

Jen started sobbing again and this time was inconsolable. Michael tried to reach out to her but she pulled away.

"Jen, I am so sorry. Please forgive me. I had no idea."

Through her tears, she snapped at him, "Don't ask me to forgive you, ask God! I could never trust you again. I've lost you forever. You have ruined everything!"

She turned and stormed back to her apartment leaving Michael standing alone in the parking lot.

From a few rows over, a classmate yelled, "Dude, what'd you do to that girl? She was mad as hell at you. Sure wouldn't want to be in your shoes!"

Michael climbed back in his truck and sped away.

For the next few weeks, he called her every day, but she wouldn't answer his calls. He went to her apartment but she wouldn't see him. If she saw him on campus, she would turn and avoid him.

Before going to sleep, he decided to make one last attempt to reach her and was surprised when her roommate answered the phone. She told Michael that Jen had been rushed to the hospital that morning with a severe headache and nausea. She didn't have any other information other than Jen had been admitted to St. Mary's and her parents were on their way.

Michael rushed to the hospital and found the Prescotts standing by her bed looking very concerned. They said Jen was extremely weak and hadn't been able to speak to them. The doctors said she had an aneurysm and they were continuing to run tests. They may not know anything for a few days.

Michael offered to stay with Jen while they got checked into a hotel. The Prescotts were reluctant to leave but agreed to let him stay. They were by Jen's side during the day but agreed to let Michael sit with her through the night because her condition had not changed. This schedule continued for three days. When Michael arrived for the nightshift, he could see that something was wrong. Mrs. Prescott was in tears and Mr. Prescott was in a serious discussion with the doctor. Jen had slipped into a coma and was unresponsive.

For the next two weeks, her condition did not improve. Each day, the Prescotts sat and prayed for their daughter's life, and each night, Michael continued to sit by her side. He waited until all of her family and visitors left for the night, then he pulled out the Bible she had given him for graduation and read to her. He wasn't sure how to talk to God, but he prayed and talked to Jen as if they both could hear him.

Two weeks later, Michael arrived for his evening stint and was ushered to a private waiting room by the Prescotts. The doctors asked them to consider taking her off life support. There was nothing more they could do and the tests showed Jen was brain dead.

All the color drained out of Michael's face as he turned to Tom Prescott and begged, "No! No, please. You can't do that. Please give her more time!"

Tom grabbed Michael's arm and said, "Don't worry, Michael. We're not going to do that. We're just praying for a miracle."

That night, the Prescotts were reluctant to leave their daughter, but Michael asked if he could be with her alone. When everyone left her room, Michael got down on his knees beside Jen's hospital bed and began begging and pleading to God.

"Please, Lord, don't take her away from me. Father, I love her so much. Father God, she loves you so much, but don't take her from me.

She's all I have. Please, please don't take her."

Michael pleaded with Jen not to go away, telling her how much he loved her and begged her not to leave him.

"Jen, I love you so much. Come back to me. Please."

Michael continued to pray and plead throughout the night, oblivious to the nurses making their rounds who left in tears hearing his despair. All night he prayed, "Don't take her. Please don't take her."

By sunrise, still on his knees, totally exhausted and half asleep, his head and arms on Jen's bed, he continued mumbling, "Jen, I love you. Don't leave me. Jen, I love you. Don't leave me."

In the quiet of the hospital room, he thought he heard a voice say, "I'll never leave you." He looked up as Jen, still weak and half conscious, squeezed his hand. He jumped to his feet, hugging and kissing her. He was laughing and crying all at once as he ran out of the room to find help.

The nurses met him in the hall and said, "We know! We saw the changes on her monitors. The doctor has been called and is on his way now."

The room was buzzing with excitement with nurses running in and out checking her vital signs while Michael stepped out to call Jen's parents. When Tom heard the emotion in Michael's voice he expected the worst possible news. Instead, Michael was crying as he shared the excitement, "Tom, Jen's okay. She's okay. She's out of the coma and she's going to be alright. Tom, she's come back to us!"

Tom called to his wife, "Virginia! Jenny woke up! Hurry, get dressed. She's okay! Oh, thank God. She's going to be okay! Michael, thank you. I'll call the boys and tell them the incredible news, and let them know she's going to be alright. We'll be right there. Thank you, Lord!"

Instead of heading back to Jen's room, Michael knew he needed to find the hospital chapel. He opened the door and entered the dimly lit room. He could almost feel the silence as he walked toward the front and knelt down. He started to pray, and as he prayed, the tears began to flow. Soon, he was crying so hard his body was shaking. He kept praying and thanking God for His mercy and for giving Jen the precious gift of life.

"Father, I will always love you. I will never doubt you again."

Michael's heart was so filled with love, he thought it would burst. He wondered if this was what Jen called the power of prayer.

When he returned to Jen's room with his face still streaked red from crying, the Prescotts were standing on either side of her bed. Jen looked up at him and said in a still weak voice, "Michael, you've been crying. Is everything alright?"

Trying to hold back the tears, he answered, "Everything is better than alright."

Jen held out her arm and Michael took her hand in both of his and kissed it, and the tears came again. The Prescotts were crying, too.

When Michael and Jen were alone, he asked her, "Do you think this has anything to do with the power of prayer?"

"Yes. I think that's exactly what it is."

"Jen, the first time I saw your face when you walked into that classroom at Brighton, my heart jumped, and I knew I wanted you in my life forever."

Jen smiled at him and said, "Michael, sit down. I have to tell you the most incredible thing that happened to me. It's unbelievable, really. When I was lying in the bed, I heard your voice calling me saying 'Jen, come back. Don't leave me.' You were telling me you loved me over and over again. I tried to come back to you. I tried so hard, but I just seemed to get farther away. Your voice was getting softer, then I heard you say 'Father, don't take her from me. She is all I have.'

"Then the strangest thing happened. I heard another voice, strong and clear but gentle say to me, "Go back to him, my child. Your time has not come.'

"In an instant, I was awake in this room, and I saw you crying next to me. Michael, I believe God heard your prayers and sent me back to you. When I awoke, I couldn't speak but I knew that I was back and that I would never leave you."

Michael just stared at her in total bewilderment.

Chapter 12: Death

"As for man, his days are like grass; he flourishes like a flower of the field; for the wind passes over it, and it is gone, and its place knows it no more." Psalm 103:15-16

During the remaining months of college, the two were inseparable, spending every free minute together. Their friends laughed and said that instead of acting like college graduates, they acted more like teenagers in love. Jen worked hard and with Michael's help was able to make up her missed work and graduate on time.

When the big day arrived, they walked hand in hand into the stadium splitting up only so that Jen could sit in the section marked "P" while Michael sat with the group marked "T".

Michael and Jen thanked their family and friends for coming to celebrate their accomplishments, waved goodbye and said they would be following soon. With the vehicles packed up, they said goodbye to Athens and everything they called home for the last four years. Their drive took them by St. Mary's, and as they passed the hospital where so much had changed for them, they both thanked God to be driving away together.

Finally, they were on their way back to Valdosta to start the next chapter of their lives. On the way, they stopped at a deli in Monticello for lunch, both ordering tuna sandwiches. Michael was paying the bill as Jen headed for the door. He called out to her, "I'll see you at the car, Honey."

Jen turned to him with a grin and said, "I told you not to call me that. I don't like it."

The waitress gave Michael a strange look and said, "What's her problem? Most girls like a handsome guy callin' them honey."

Michael smiled and said, "Believe me, she is not like most girls. She's something special."

Michael followed Jen to her house to help unpack her car before heading to The Farm where the Judge was waiting for him. As they drove down the familiar road to the Prescott's house, they saw that the entire area had been transformed. There were lights strung from trees, tables loaded with food, balloons and banners welcoming them home, and it looked like everyone they cared about was there to greet them.

Jen jumped out of her car, ran to hug her parents and the twins, then greeted the other guests while Michael leaned against his truck, shaking his head and taking in the festivities around him. He spotted Billy and B.J. in the crowd and walked over to them hugging them both. An adorable two year old girl was shyly holding onto her daddy's leg while B.J. held a baby in her arms.

Michael stayed at the party for a few hours catching up with his old friends. He thanked the Prescotts for the warm welcome back and headed home to The Farm.

He hadn't been back often since his grandmother died. It didn't seem right being there without her. As he traveled down the long, familiar driveway, he missed Jen already. Only Mae Belle was waiting for him when he drove up to the house.

"Oh, Michael. It's so good to see you. Now go on inside. The Judge is waitin' for you in the library. I'll have Charley help get your things up to your room."

Michael walked into the Judge's domain with all its familiar sights and smells and was greeted with, "Well, boy, you are finally home. Now we can get down to business."

"Hi, Papa. Nice to see you, too. I just got here, and I thought I'd take some time off before I start working."

"No time to waste, Boy. I'm glad you're finished with school, but your real education starts Monday."

Reluctantly, Michael accompanied the Judge to the Enterprise headquarters early Monday morning and was greeted by the executive officers and the administrative staff who were already there to welcome him and wish him well.

The Judge turned to Sally, his personal assistant, and said, "Call a mandatory meeting in the conference room at 11:00, and make sure Bill Baxter and Walter are there. Michael and I will be in our office and are not to be disturbed until then."

Michael did not miss the "our office" reference. The next few hours were spent reviewing contracts and discussing details.

When they walked into the conference room together, all of the executives seated around the table immediately stopped talking. The Judge introduced everyone by name and position and gave a brief background of each person.

The Judge said, "As you know, my grandson, Michael, has been away at school, but now his real education starts." Everyone laughed respectfully as the Judge continued, "From now on, I want Michael to be informed of everything pertaining to the Tillman Enterprise. Is that clear?"

Bill Baxter spoke up, "Does that include the Con-tech merger and the Merling Company take-over?"

"I said 'everything'. I want Michael to know what I know. He will be working out of my office, and I will be transitioning my position so eventually I'll be in the office from around 10-2. For the time being, everything will remain the same."

When they returned to their shared office, Michael looked at the Judge and said, "Papa, there's no way I can run the whole Enterprise and The Farm. It's too much. I just can't do it."

The Judge glared at Michael, "I don't ever want to hear you say 'I can't'! Do you understand, Boy? Now sit down and listen to everything I say. When I was 18, my father died and left me with 10,000 acres of woods, a few hundred acres of cotton and tobacco, two saw mills, two small companies and two apartment houses. All I knew was a little about farming tobacco and cotton, and I had very little education. I was 18, had a sixteen year old wife and a baby on the way. I didn't have the luxury of saying 'I can't do it'. I took over the business then started college. I learned as I went, finished college then grad school and eventually becoming the most powerful man in town."

The next day, and every day from then on, Michael was at the office at seven and didn't leave until seven in the evening. Jen and Michael made a priority to see each other every weekend and as often as possible for dinner. Michael secured a position for Jen in the accounting department at Tillman where she wanted to work a few years before taking the CPA exam.

For the next nine months, things ran smoothly, and Michael was learning more about the Enterprise each day. On a busy Tuesday morning, Michael looked up from his paperwork and noticed the time. It was 10:20, and his grandfather had not yet arrived at the office. He thought that was odd but assumed he must be delayed with farm business. He was about to dig back into some legal documents when Bill Baxter, Walter and Sally walked into his office. This trio didn't usually arrive together and certainly not without scheduling something first. He could see that this was not going to be good.

Bill Baxter spoke first, "Michael, we have some bad news. The Judge died in his sleep last night. Mae Belle found him dead this morning. She called you, but Sally took the call, came to me, and the three of us wanted to tell you together."

Sally was crying, "Michael, we are so sorry. We will miss him so much."

Jen came running into the office and hugged Michael.

"I'm so sorry, Michael. Mae Belle just called me and I hurried over as quickly as I could."

Michael said, "Thanks, Jen. Thanks to all of you. Jen, we need to go to the farm right now. Bill, I will call you later."

When they arrived at the farm, the ambulance was in the driveway with the Judge's body inside. There were also two police cars and the county coroner's van parked in front of the house.

One of the police officers came over to tell Michael he was sorry for his loss and remarked that the Judge was a great man. The officers said they were finished and were ready to leave unless Michael needed them for anything. He discussed with the coroner where to take the body of his grandfather and walked into the empty house.

The funeral was held four days later, and there were over two hundred people at the burial site to pay their respects. A few people spoke about their relationship with the Judge and Bill Baxter presented a plaque to be mounted on the tombstone. He read the engraved inscription:

Here lies a great man.

He built an empire.

He did it his way.

Everyone applauded except for Michael who stood solemnly with a grimace on his face. The pastor asked if he would like to say a few words.

Michael stood by the grave and said, "Yes, people say my grandfather was a great man. However, he was also..."

Michael stopped speaking and tried again, "He was. . ."

He stopped and said, "I'm sorry."

Michael walked back to Jen and took her hand, squeezing it. She said, "It's alright, darling."

The congregation sang Amazing Grace and the pastor thanked everyone for coming. Michael and Jen stood alone by the grave of his grandfather. He looked over and saw the elaborate tombstones for his grandmother and parents. He slowly turned away and started walking back to the car. Instead of leaving, he kept walking and continued on to a part of the cemetery that wasn't as grand or well maintained.

He stopped at Matty's grave and knelt down beside it, touching the simple marker.

Michael said to Jen, "You know, my grandfather never did anything for anyone if it didn't benefit him. He would use people. He'd buy companies, sell the assets to make a bunch of money, send it into bankruptcy without any regard for the people who had worked there for years then take a tax write-off. He never gave a thought about the people who lost their livelihoods. Just think, over two hundred people showed up for his funeral. Matty here, a poor black woman, loved, raised and cared for a spoiled little white kid. She gave up her life for me.

"My grandmother used to give old clothes and furniture to Matty, and she would turn around and give them to the people she knew needed it more. She did so much for people, but when she died, there were only eight people at her funeral.

"Their lives were so different. Why was my grandfather called a great man when he really wasn't one? I don't want to be remembered as being great but know in my heart it's not true?"

Michael shook his head and sadly said, "So they show up for him

because he's rich and powerful. Like
that means something?"

"No, Michael, they came for
you. Because you are a great man."

Jen held his hand as they
walked back to the car in silence.

Chapter 13: Family

"Then the man said, "This at last is bone of my bone and flesh of my flesh, she shall be called woman, because she was taken out of a man." Genesis 2:23

Two weeks after his grandfather was buried, Michael and Jen rode back out to Lonesome Pine. There, he proposed to her with his mother's ring, and they started planning their special day.

Since Jen's miraculous recovery, the two had been attending a Catholic Church together, and it only seemed right that they should get married at St. Johns. They spoke with the priest about the service, discussing what they wanted and how many people they expected. Jen wanted it to be a small wedding with just family and close friends, but

Michael hoped to share the special occasion with everyone they knew.

Three days later, Jen and Michael were discussing their wedding plans over dinner. They had been attending the Catholic Church, so they agreed that was where they should be married even though it was small and only seated about two hundred people.

Jen was concerned, "Michael, I was thinking of a small, modest wedding."

Michael replied, "Sweetheart, I'm afraid it will be anything but small and modest. The Church holds a few hundred and there will likely be another hundred or so standing outside. I'm sure there will be at least four hundred people coming to the reception."

"Oh, Michael, my parents can't afford to feed four hundred people!"

"I know, Jen, but under the circumstances, maybe they will let me……I'm sorry, I mean us…..pay for the reception."

When the big day finally arrived, the wedding turned out to be perfect, and Jen was a stunning bride as they started their life together.

Billy stood with Michael at the altar as his best man, and Jen's four brothers were at his side as well. Jen's best friends from high school and college wore off the shoulder floor length dresses in pale blue, and Billy's daughter carried a basket of rose petals down the center aisle.

A few months later, they found out they were expecting their first child. Michael was ecstatic and could talk of nothing else. He read books and asked for advice from everyone at work. They warned him about morning sickness, mood swings and strange food cravings, but the first few months went along with ease.

He was expecting to sail through the next few months without any difficulties until one night Jen woke Michael up at 2 AM with a strange request.

"Michael, I really want some chocolate ice cream. Would you mind running to the store to get some?"

"Sure, Jen. I'll be happy to pick some up on the way back from work tomorrow, or you can send Mae Belle out in the morning."

"Um, no. I mean now. I really need some ice cream now. And maybe some pickles."

"Jen, its 2:00 in the morning! Where am I supposed to get those things at this hour? I'm sure you'll still want them tomorrow. Can't it wait?"

Jen started crying, "You don't care about me. You don't love me anymore because I'm getting fat and when I walk I waddle like a duck."

Michael smiled and said, "I love the way you waddle!"

Jen looked at him and started crying harder.

"I'm so sorry, Jen. Please stop crying, Sweetheart. You know I love you more than anything in the world. I'll go right now and get whatever you want."

As Michael ran out the door, Jen yelled, "Don't forget the pickles!"

Michael drove into town and found a store that was still opened.

He picked out her special requests and headed to the register to pay.

The cashier smiled at him and said, "Pregnant, right?"

Michael sighed and said, "You got it."

When Michael returned home, he called out to Jen but got no answer. He went in search of her hoping to cheer her up with the late night snack and found Jen sound asleep in their room sprawled out across the bed. He covered her up with a blanket and grabbed another for himself and spent the night on the sofa in his office.

The next morning, Michael walked into the kitchen where Jen was already seated at the table, ice cream and pickles in front of her.

Mae Belle poured Michael a cup of coffee and told him the eggs and bacon would be ready in a few minutes.

"That's alright, Mae Belle. I'll just get something on the way to the office."

He finished his coffee and kissed his wife on the top of her head, and as he glanced back at her sitting there, no make-up, hair in disarray, dressed in his old flannel shirt with a pickle in one hand, the juice running down her chin, and a spoonful of ice cream in the other, he thought that his beautiful wife had lost her mind. He smiled at her and left for the office.

The strange cravings continued, but Michael learned to be prepared so he could avoid any more late night shopping trips. As Jen's belly grew larger, she talked to the baby and played classical music all day. Jen already felt connected because she felt him kick and move and knew when he was sleeping or was restless. She started loving him before she could even see his face.

Michael couldn't understand the connection she felt with their child and was afraid he wouldn't be able to experience that level of love and devotion to the baby. It didn't take long for him to discover that he was in for the most wonderful experience of his life, something that would change his life forever.

Michael received a frantic call from Jen one morning when he was at the office telling him Mae Belle was rushing her to the hospital. It was time.

"I'm on my way. I'll meet you there. Don't have the baby until I get there!"

Through her contractions she said mockingly, "Sure, Michael, we'll wait until you get here."

The Prescotts beat him to the hospital and were with Jen when he arrived. The nurses took Jen and Michael to labor and delivery where they soon greeted their baby boy. The nurse placed the tiny baby in Michael's arms, and when he looked at the beautiful face of the little miracle he held, he knew he would gladly give his life for him. He finally understood the connection Jen felt for all those months she carried him.

Michael studied the tiny features of his face and his small hands and feet. The baby made a few small noises and stretched his arms to the delight of his father. He turned to Jen with tears in his eyes and said, "Thank you."

They decided to name their son, Michael with the nickname Chip, and he was definitely a "chip off the old block". Michael was enamored with him. He didn't think it was possible, but his love for Chip grew even more each day.

Michael could hardly wait to get home in the evening and cherished the time with Chip on the weekends. He loved helping with bath-time, feeding, even diaper changes. He sang songs, told stories and put him to bed. By the time Chip could walk, he and Michael were inseparable.

Being a new father made him re-evaluate the important things in his life. He spent many restless nights thinking about the businesses he inherited from his grandfather and how he fit into it all. After a long weekend of reflecting, he came to the office with a plan.

He asked Sally to call a meeting with Bill and Walter as soon as possible. When they entered the conference room, Michael jumped right into it.

"I have decided to make some significant changes around here."

The men stirred in their seats and glanced at each other nervously.

Michael sensed the tension and quickly put them at ease.

With a smile, he said, "Don't worry. It has nothing to do with you. I have given this a lot of thought, and I want to change the basic philosophy of Tillman Enterprises. Going forward, we will not buy up failing companies just to gain any profits we can then take a write-off when they fail. I'm not willing to put people out of work for our gain."

"I want to continue aggressively going after these failing companies, and I want us to invest in them, to bring them back to successful, profitable operation."

Bill looked concerned and spoke up, "Michael, I understand how you feel, but this is not wise and certainly not a good business practice. It takes a lot of time and money to build up a weak company.

The Judge never would have approved of this"

"Bill, I am not my grandfather. This is my company now, and I will run it the way I think best. I have given this a great deal of thought. I also want to re-evaluate the benefits packages we offer all the employees on our payroll and discuss profit sharing as well."

"One more thing, Bill. I want you to get with the legal department and have them draw up the necessary paperwork for me to sign. If for some reason I am unable to run the Enterprise, I want Jen to legally have all the power and authority I have to run the business."

"Certainly, Michael. I will get started on that right away."

During the next three year, Michael learned more about the operation of the business and his changes to the corporate structure were proving to be very profitable. He put in long hours but slipped away as often as possible to spend time with his family.

Chapter 14: Grief

"My joy is gone; grief is upon me; my heart is sick within me." Jeremiah 8:18

It seemed that everything in his life was perfect. The company was thriving, and he adored Jen and Chip. He could never have imagined how quickly things would change.

One morning, Michael was running late for a meeting and rushed downstairs, kissing Jen on the way to the car.

"Love you, Sweetheart. I'll see you and the Chipper tonight."

As he rushed out of the house, he left the front door slightly ajar. Michael didn't realize that Chip was awake when he left, but his son didn't want to miss the chance to give his daddy a kiss goodbye.

At the same time, Jen noticed Michael's briefcase sitting on the hall table. She grabbed it and ran to the front door just as Michael started backing out of the driveway, not realizing Chip was behind the car.

She ran out, screaming for him to stop, but it was too late.

He jumped out of the car to Jen's screaming, "Oh my god! What have you done, Michael! You have killed our baby!"

Michael pulled Chip from under the car, blood pouring from his nose and mouth. He held the lifeless body of his precious son in his arms, clutching him to his chest, as Jen knelt down beside him in shock. She begged Michael to give Chip to her, but he couldn't hear anything she said. He held the fragile body, willing him to breathe, but it was too late.

It seemed like an eternity, but Michael finally broke out of his shock and started yelling for help. They were both in utter disbelief. Mae Belle heard the noise and ran outside, seeing the horror in front of her, she ran back inside and called 911.

The paramedics arrived quickly. Mae Belle tried to comfort Jen while Charley, rushing from the barn, held Michael back while the emergency personnel worked on Chip. As they looked on in horror, they were overcome with grief and the intense mental and emotional pain brought on by this sudden tragedy.

Mae Belle went back inside the house and called the Prescotts, knowing Jen would need them now. She also called Sally.

The police soon arrived followed by the Prescotts, and the tiny body was covered with a blanket. An officer helped Michael to the front steps of the house and sat with him as he asked the unpleasant details of the horrific accident.

Michael and Jen were numb in the days that followed, barely going through the motions as their family and friends helped with the funeral arrangements.

Three days later, they were back at St. John's Church. It was hard to believe their lives together began at this church, and now their world was falling apart. Jen was able to hold herself together as she greeted the mourners who offered their sympathy and condolences, but Michael was catatonic, unable to respond to anyone.

When services concluded at the gravesite and everyone had left except for their close friends and family, Michael remained by the small casket, unwilling to leave his son. No amount of persuasion from the Prescotts or Billy and B.J. could convince him to move from that spot.

Finally, Billy offered to stay with him and said he would bring Michael home whenever he was ready. The two friends sat in silence, Michael in a catatonic state of grief, and Billy in fervent prayer for his childhood friend.

After a few hours, Billy finally managed to help Michael into the car. They drove a short distance with Michael staring out the passenger side window at the passing landscape but seeing nothing.

He said softly, "Billy, Chip never had a chance to go to school and make friends. He never had a chance to grow up and fall in love. He never had a chance to do

anything. Why? Billy, I don't
understand why?"

Billy wasn't sure how to
respond to someone he loved like a
brother who had suffered so much
loss in his life. As he drove in
silence praying for the right words,
Michael continued, "Turn around. We
have to go back. There's no one with
him, and Chip is afraid of the
dark."

Billy couldn't respond as tears
were streaming down his face. He
drove slowly back to The Farm,
knowing that Michael's grief was
only just beginning.

As the weeks went by, Michael
rarely spoke and never mentioned
Chip. He was burdened by the intense
guilt he felt and was devastated by
their loss. He tried his best to
avoid Jen, only speaking to her out
of necessity and usually with a
short, brusque reply.

Michael spent many hours alone
in the library drinking heavily to
help mask the pain. Jen, working
though her own grief, was worried
about Michael's mental state and the
state of their marriage. She even

tried on a few occasions to suggest they seek counseling together, but he would have none of it.

Jen became steadily frustrated with Michael as he refused to speak with friends or return to work, and his attitude toward her worsened. Billy stopped by often but was constantly told it wasn't a good time. Sally called to check on Michael daily, but he refused to take her calls.

Eventually, Michael emerged from his office, showered and dressed and told Jen he was heading out for a little while. She was encouraged, assuming he was finally going to the office. It was the first time he had left the house in months, and this seemed like a positive sign. She discovered it was just the opposite.

When he didn't return by dinnertime, she called Sally, but he never arrived at work. She was terrified, assuming the worst. He finally returned home at 2 AM drunk and disheveled, and this pattern continued for the next few weeks. There was nothing Jen could say that helped the situation, and her pleading with him actually made things worse.

He began snapping at her whenever she asked where he had been and replied that it was none of her business. She prayed for him and for the right words to get through, but none of her pleading seemed to matter. He ignored her when she said his behavior was destroying his life and their marriage.

After months of watching him fall apart, Jen finally mentioned their son.

"Michael, Chip was my son, too. The pain I feel is beyond comprehension, but we need each other to get through our loss. We are called to bury the dead not to let the dead bury us."

Michael snapped at her, "Jen, don't you understand? I will never get over this. I don't want to work through this! Can't you get it through your head? I killed our son!"

"Oh, Michael. You are so wrong. It was a horrible accident. It wasn't your fault."

"Don't ever talk to me about this again. I don't need you to tell me it's all going to be okay. I'm sick of hearing your constant nagging. I don't need you to tell me when to come home or how to behave. I don't need you in my life! Just leave me alone. I'm leaving and I won't be back."

As Michael drove away, Jen stood alone in the doorway staring out into the darkness, seeing nothing, hearing nothing, feeling nothing. She had tried so hard to keep everything together for Michael's sake but now he was gone. She remained there in a state of shock, unable to comprehend what had just transpired. Had Michael really left her forever?

She stared into the emptiness unaware that it has started raining. She kept running the last few months over and over in her head, wondering what she had done to make him hate her so much and what she could have done to make him happy again.

As she stood in the doorway, an unusual feeling came over her, something she had never experienced

before. The joy and peace she
normally felt were replaced with
intense anger and bitterness.

Jen eased the door closed
behind her and headed back into the
quiet and empty house. She slowly
walked into the dining room, and
without thinking, grabbed a crystal
vase from the sideboard and hurled
it with all her strength at the
front door.

The vase exploded into hundreds
of tiny pieces as she sank trembling
and sobbing to the floor. She looked
up and screamed, "Michael was right!
You are a mean and hateful God! Why
did you do this to us? Why did you
hurt Michael so much? He tried so
hard to know you. All he wanted was
to learn how to love you, but you
took his mother and father when he
was a scared little boy. You took
Matty when he desperately needed
someone to love him. Now you've
taken his son who he adored and
killed our marriage, too! What more
do you want from him?"

Exhausted and scared, Jen
crawled to the living room sofa and
passed out from the emotional

turmoil, but her sleep was restless and troubled. She worried about Michael in his current condition. She was uneasy and regretful for her angry outburst toward God, and she felt total despair and loneliness.

Curled up on the sofa in pain, Jen began feeling an odd sense of peace. She gradually began to realize what she knew all of her life and what she constantly shared with others. When trials and tribulations confront us, no matter how hard they seem, it is God's mysterious way of opening new doors to give us opportunities and insights that would otherwise never be presented to us.

As the pain lessened, Jen thought of the teachings that spiritual growth often occurs out of our worst tragedies with God's help and the working of the Holy Spirit. Jen also knew that tragedy often prepares our hearts for ministry to others going through tribulation.

Jen got on her knees and prayed, "Father, I realize now that this was a time in my life that I really needed you and I failed to accept your love for me. I know there are times when only you can help us. Please use my pain for your glory. This hurts so much, but I know you have a plan for me. It feels like nothing will take away this pain. It is so overwhelming. I know that no one can help me but you. Father, I ask your forgiveness for my anger and lack of faith, and I ask your will be done in my life."

Jen went back to sleep, and for the first time in months, it was peaceful and undisturbed. She awoke the next morning and knew that with God's help she could handle whatever He had planned for her future.

Chapter 15: Fear

"The fear of man lays a snare, but whoever trusts in the Lord is safe." Proverbs 29:25

As he professed, Michael didn't return home. Jen spent the next few days wandering around the empty house and riding out to Lonesome Pine to think and pray.

Her father suggested she meet with the executive board at the Enterprise to let them know what was happening and to see if they could offer any help. She told Bill Baxter everything that had happened since the funeral, about Michael's late nights out and heavy drinking. She knew he was spending a lot of money and thought maybe he was taking drugs as well.

Bill listened intently and was concerned for Michael and Jen but also for the company.

"The first thing we have to do is cut off his supply of money. I can see to that today. If we cut off his personal and business accounts and he has no access to money, maybe he'll come to his senses. We need to stop him from throwing money around foolishly. There are a lot of people counting on him, and we have to look out for their interests, too."

Bill continued, "I thought it was unnecessary at the time, but after the Judge died, Michael made provisions in case anything happened to him or if he was unable to run the daily operation of the Enterprise for you to have full legal authority as acting president. I drew up the papers myself, so I know they are legal and binding. You need to come back to work but not in accounting. You'll need to start working here as the acting president. It's important for Michael and for you. It would do you a world of good to get away from The Farm."

"Bill, it probably would be good for me, but I'm going to need a lot of help. I have no idea how to even begin running a company like this."

"Don't worry. Walter and I taught Michael, and we can teach you, too. Of course, Sally knows everything that's going on around here, and she'll be a huge help to you."

"Okay. I'll start tomorrow morning."

Bill smiled, "Eight o'clock sharp."

"I'll be here."

When Michael discovered his access to money was cut-off, he was furious but couldn't do anything about it. He had been living in a cheap motel, spending money on alcohol, gambling and the wild life he hoped would take his mind off his grief.

The only item of any value he took with him when he sped away from Jen was his Ford pickup truck worth about $25,000. Without the title that was filed away at his office, he had no choice but to sell to a shady used car dealer for $5,000.

Michael quickly burned through the cash, and feeling like he had nowhere else to turn, started living on the street. At first, he was ashamed to be seen wandering the streets during the day in case someone from his previous life saw him in his current condition. He looked for discarded food behind restaurants at night, but after he was beaten up and mugged a few times, he started scrounging for food during the day.

He had fallen so low that he was no longer afraid of being seen wandering the streets. He even began begging for food and money for drugs and alcohol.

Billy went in search of Michael many times, but he always refused to go back with him. It broke Billy's heart to tell Jen of Michael's condition, but they both continued to pray for him and trust that God was watching out for him.

It had been almost a year, and Michael was in an abyss where nothing mattered and he no longer cared if he lived or died. As Michael was wandering the streets, a few of his old acquaintances from the pool hall days in high school saw him sitting next to an abandoned building.

They spoke with him for a few minutes, but Michael shared nothing of the events that brought him to this place. They offered Michael a way of making a lot of money, and he told them he was interested. They worked with a bookie betting on college football games. They didn't have any money to place a bet, but with the Tillman name, Michael could easily place the bet for them and they'd split the winnings with him.

It sounded like an easy enough way to get some cash, so in his muddled mind from alcohol and drugs, he agreed to the plan. They would use his name to bet $10,000 on two games. Of course, there was no downside for them. If they won, great. If they lost, it was Michael's neck on the line.

The next day, both teams lost, and Michael was now in debt to the bookies for $20,000. His former friends suggested that he double down as a last ditch effort to get some money for themselves. Again, it seemed like a reasonable idea to Michael, so he agreed.

He lost that bet as well and was told he now owed $40,000 and payment was due Monday. His friends pretended to be sorry about it, and Michael barely understood the significance of what they were telling him. They said if he didn't pay on time, the bookie would probably kill him. When the pool hall boys realized they weren't likely to get any money from Michael, they felt only slightly sorry for him and suggested he leave town or hide.

Without money, Michael couldn't go anywhere, and he didn't know what to do. He didn't want to call Jen or Billy because he had hit such a low place in his life, and he wanted to keep them out of it.

As he stumbled behind some abandoned buildings, he found a sewage pipe that emptied into a holding pond for a treatment plant. He stayed in the pipe throughout the night, and as his head cleared, he realized he needed Billy's help after all. If he could get to Billy, he could hopefully get the money he needed to leave town.

It took some time, but Michael was able to jump on an empty train car that took him close enough to Swamp Road that he could walk the rest of the way to Billy's house. Mrs. Dean died several years ago and left the house to Billy and B.J. who lived there with their two children. Fortunately, B.J. and the children were not home when Michael, in his filth, knocked on the front door.

Billy was shocked when he opened the door and saw his best friend standing there.

"My god, Michael! I'm so glad to see you. What the hell happened? You look like you've been wallowing in a sewer. And, man, you smell like it, too."

He asked Michael to hose off at the side of the house and said he would be right back. Billy returned with a wash cloth, soap, a trash bag and some towels. He asked Michael to take his clothes and shoes and throw them in the bag.

After he had cleaned up, Michael came in the house wrapped in a towel. Billy asked him to go to the bathroom and shower again and shave.

"Scrub yourself good with this bottle of disinfectant and clean your head. You probably have bugs in your hair! I'll find you some clothes and shoes then I'll fix us something to eat. We need to talk."

Michael told Billy the whole story, about all the months he spend living on the street and the money he owed the bookies. Billy's heart broke for everything Michael had endured.

"Man, you really are in deep trouble. These guys don't mess around, and they're going to want every penny you owe them. It won't help to run because they'll find you anywhere. You won't be able to come back until they get their money."

Billy thought about it and continued, "I have a better idea. You remember the moonshine cabin way back in the swamp where we used to go when we were kids? They would never find you there."

He put together some food and water, a kerosene lamp, flash light, radio, mosquito repellent and some blankets. He also gave Michael a pistol and shot gun and said, "In case of critters."

Billy promised to come by every few days to check on him and bring more food and water.

In the meantime, the bookies made their way to The Farm and questioned Jen about Michael's location. She didn't know where he was, and she was distressed that a bunch of rough looking guys were looking for him.

They told her he owed them money, and they weren't going to stop looking for him. She knew he was in serious trouble.

"If I pay the money, will you leave him alone?"

"All we want is our $40Gs and we don't care who gives it to us. We don't want to hurt you or him. If you give us the money, you won't see us again."

"I'll need a few days, but I'll get your money."

"We'll be back in two days."

As soon as they left, Jen rushed to the office and met with

Bill Baxter to tell him what was happening. She told Bill that Michael was still missing, but if the bookies didn't get paid, they were going to hurt him.

Bill Baxter helped her get the money together, and two days later, she handed over a stack of bills, paying his debt in full.

Billy stopped by The Farm to check on Jen and warn her about the people who may be coming around looking for Michael and a payoff.

"Yes, they were here already, and I gave them the money."

"Then it's safe for him to come home?"

"Billy, do you know where Michael is? Is he alright?"

Billy hugged Jen and said, "I'll bring him home right now."

Billy made his way through the swamp, as Michael, sober and off drugs, began to pray that his nightmare would be over. He didn't know how to pay his way out of the mess he made and he didn't know where to go. He just wanted to go home.

He knelt on the floor by the cot and prayed for deliverance. He heard a strong and clear voice say, "Michael, it's time to go home."

Michael looked around the cabin, but he was alone. He searched the cabin, but no one was there. He looked out the window as Billy's boat was nearing the cabin.

Billy yelled up to him, "Michael, it's okay! It's all over. You can go home now."

Billy walked in the cabin and hugged Michael.

"I talked to Jen. She's at home waiting for you. It's time for you to go home."

Michael smiled at him and felt hope for the first time since the tragedy.

Billy looked at him and shook his head, "You're not going back to Jen looking like that. Let's stop by my house so you can shower again. Maybe B.J. can cut your hair. You look like crap."

As Billy drove him back to The Farm, Michael thought of how unkind and selfish he had been and wondered if Jen would ever forgive him for abandoning her. He knew she had been in horrible pain, too, but he thought only of his own despair. With apprehension, he looked at the house and hoped they would eventually be able to reconcile and this would again be a happy place. Before Billy could stop the car, the front door swung open wide and Jen came running down the steps with tears streaming down her face. Michael jumped out of the car, barely giving Billy time to stop, and desperately ran to Jen. They enveloped each other as if they were holding onto a lifeline, kissing passionately. Billy stepped out of the car and stood in silence as he witnessed two souls coming together again after so much heartache and loss. He drove away with gratitude for the remarkable reunion. As Michael and Jen embraced, the painful months passed away.

He was finally home.

Chapter 16: Healing

"And he went throughout all Galilee teaching in their synagogues and proclaiming the gospel of the kingdom and healing every disease and every affliction among the people." Matthew 4:23

Michael and Jen talked late into the night. They shared the pain of the nightmare they recently endured and agreed they would get through it together. They also decided that Michael should get professional help to clean up his life.

A few days later, Michael was admitted into a rehabilitation facility specializing in alcohol and drugs abuse. They recommended a therapy that would require him to stay focused without visitors for the first few weeks. After that, he could have guests for a few hours on the weekend. Eventually, he would be allowed to go home on the weekends until he was ready to be dismissed from the facility.

Before Michael's first home visit, Jen met with the doctors to get advice about how to make the transition the most successful, to find out if there were things she should avoid discussing with him. They suggested she should act naturally and keep things as normal as possible. This would be a test for how well he was adjusting and reacting to everyday situations.

When they arrived at The Farm for the first weekend visit, Michael got out of the car hesitantly, looking around the parking area and pushing the horrific memories out of his head. He took Jen's hand and they walked into the house together. Mae Belle hugged Michael and welcomed him home.

Michael and Jen sat on the porch watching the sun set over the fields and talked about his treatment and how things were going at the Enterprise. For the first time in over a year, they talked about their future and had hope.

Jen led him upstairs to their room, with candles lit and a bath drawn, they remembered what it was like to be husband and wife again. That night they fell asleep in each others arms.

After a light breakfast the next morning, they packed up their well-worn picnic basket and headed down to the stable where the horses were saddled and waiting for them. It was a beautiful, clear day, as they spread their blanket under the old oak by the lake.

Michael was quiet for a while and finally said, "Jen, I'm afraid with everything that's happened, I've lost my faith in God."

"I know if feels like he's abandoned you sometimes, but that is not true. Even the apostles who lived with Jesus for two years had trouble with their faith sometimes. In Luke 17:5, the apostles said to the Lord, 'Increase our faith" and the Lord replied, 'If you have faith like a grain of mustard seed, you could say to the mulberry tree, be uprooted and planted in the sea, and it would obey you'. Faith is a powerful thing.

Jen continued, "Remember in Matthew 14 verses 28-32, when Peter tried to walk on water? He was afraid and began to sink then cried out to Jesus, 'Lord, save me'. Jesus took hold of him saying, 'Oh ye of little faith, why did you doubt?' You have to understand that doubting is normal. It doesn't mean you've lost your relationship with God."

Seeing that she was slowly getting through to him, she continued, "In 1 Corinthians, Paul wrote, 'So now faith, hope and love abide, but the greatest of these is love'. And Michael, you have more love in you than anyone I know."

She reached over and squeezed his hand, "Faith is complicated. It's hard to get our minds around it. Sometimes it seems so strong and our walk is easy and other times we wonder if we have faith at all. I think it's at the times when our faith is the weakest that the Lord is carrying us the most.

The next weekend visit was much like the first. They spent hours walking hand in hand around the estate and sharing their hearts. As they walked, Michael asked, "Jen, can you explain how the Holy Spirit fits into everything?"

"Well, you know, the Holy Spirit is the third part of the Trinity. It's the first to awaken our faith and to communicate to us, to be our mentor and coach in all parts of our lives, not just in times of conflict. The difficulty is learning how to distinguish the voice of the Holy Spirit over all the other voices in our lives. You can imagine the Holy Spirit like a wall around you, keeping you safe, or a warm blanket holding you close when you're overwhelmed with life. Because of the Holy Spirit, we are empowered to make the right decisions, to forgive, to love unconditionally. The Holy Spirit helps us to renew our minds to the truth of what God says in his word and to start replacing old patterns with new ones. The Holy Spirit is at work with the Father and Son from the beginning to the completion with the divine plan of our salvation."

Michael and Jen spent the next day together preparing to have guests. They cooked a large pot of spaghetti to serve with bread and salad, and they baked a few apple pies for dessert. That evening was their first night of entertaining in a very long time. They invited the Prescotts and Deans over to join them. Everyone commented on the delicious meal, but they were most happy to see that Michael appeared to be back to his old self.

Billy raised his water glass and toasted the return of the Prodigal Son.

Michael said, "You know, I've always heard that reference to the Prodigal Son, but I don't think I've ever heard the actual story about it."

Billy spoke up, "There was a father with two sons. The father was very rich and owned a huge farm. In a parable like this, you equate the earthly father to our heavenly father. So, the younger son decided he no longer wanted to work the land, and he wanted his father to give him his inheritance right away which would have been about half of what he owned. His father tried to talk his son out of leaving but to no avail. The father finally gave in to his son's request and allowed him to leave, taking a large amount of money with him. The young man foolishly squandered all his money on drinking, gambling and wild, reckless living. Finally, he ran out of money. He tried to get a job, but no one would hire him. He eventually found a job working for a pig farmer. He was allowed to live with the pigs and eat what the pigs ate. The young man realized how sinful his behavior was and he decided to go home to ask for his father's forgiveness. He was willing to work any menial job his father would give him just to be accepted again. When the father saw his son, dirty and disheartened, walking down the road toward home, he ran to him, wrapping his arms around his son, and welcoming him home. He called for his servants to prepare a large meal to celebrate the return of his son who had been lost to him. The father forgave the son just as our heavenly Father will forgive us when we stray."

Jen spoke up, "If you analyze this story a little further, it's not only a story of two sons, one taking his inheritance and leaving his father and the other one remaining behind but refusing to accept his brother's return home because of his jealousy and anger. The rest of the story is about the love of the father for his son who turned away from him. The father never stopped loving his son, never stopped looking for him to return home.

She continued, "One day, as the father was watching and hoping for his son to return, he saw a figure appear in the distance. He continued to watch with hopeful anticipation when he realized it was truly his son. He was elated and didn't wait for his son to continue on his journey home. Instead, the father ran as fast as he could, holding up his robe so he wouldn't stumble, and yelling for the household servants to follow after him.

"What a sight that must have been! When the father reached his beloved son, he hugged and kissed him with an outpouring of joy and love. The son, on the other hand, could hardly face his father. He could only say, 'Father, I have sinned against heaven and before you.'"

"The father answered this by telling the servants to bring the best robe and put it on him. By doing so, it showed that the father understood his son was repentant and was now worthy to wear the robe."

"The son said to his father, 'I am not worthy to be called your son' but the father ordered his servants to bring the priceless family ring and place it on his son's hand, indicating he was once again a part of the family. He ordered sandals to be brought for his son's feet as only servants went without shoes.

"When the older son came home, he discovered a huge celebration for his lost brother who had returned, and he was furious, refusing to participate in the joyous event. His father came to him and entreated him to forgive his brother who was dead but now was alive; was lost but now was found."

Jen looked at Michael and said, "This parable is about the love of our father in heaven for us. No matter how much we stray; no matter how much we sin and turn away from him, he will always put the royal robe on us and a ring on our finger for we were once lost but are found, and it is a joyous occasion for our heavenly father."

Michael looked down at his empty plate and said, "That story is about me."

Jen took his hand and replied, "It's about all His children. At times, we all choose to go our own way, without guidance from God."

Tom Prescott looked at Michael and said, "Sometimes I think you're story is more like Job. I'm not sure if you're familiar with it, but it's about another rich man who was blameless and upright. He feared God and turned away from evil. He had seven sons and three daughters, and each morning, Job offered burnt sacrifices to God to atone for his children's sins.

Tom continued," Job owned huge amounts of livestock: sheep, camels, donkeys, oxen, and he had many servants. One day, the Lord said, 'Job is a most righteous man on earth.' But Satan said, 'Why not, he has everything.' God replied, 'Job would remain righteous even if I took it all away from him.' Satan did not believe it, so God sent robbers to take all Job owned. He then sent a tornado to destroy his house where his children were killed. Job had lost everything but he continued to be a righteous man. He refused to find fault with God even though he felt he had been treated unjustly. He understood that God had his reasons and a plan for his life. In the end, God restored all that He had taken away from Job and gave him much more than he first had."

Michael said sadly, "I think I'm more like the Prodigal son than Job. I'm afraid my faith has suffered through everything that's happened in my life and I'm being punished for it."

Jen spoke up, "These stories deal with the question of faith in a sovereign God. Is He good and just in His rule of the world? The stories show that the reasons for human suffering often remain secret to us. Not all troubles are punishment for wrongdoing. It isn't necessary for our faith to understand God's reasons for events in our lives."

Chapter 17: Joy

"These things I have spoken to you, that my joy may be in you, and that your joy may be full." John 15:11

When Michael was finally released from the treatment facility, his welcome home was a day to remember. Jen hoped he would sleep late so the party planning overseen by Billy could take place outside without his knowledge, but he woke up early, anxious to get back to his previous routine.

She was desperately trying to keep him occupied as she grabbed a pillow and playfully hit him in the head with it. He looked at her in shock then started laughing, grabbing his pillow and hitting her in the back. She giggled and hit him again. They continued playing until Michael got distracted

He heard a noise outside and started walking toward the bedroom window as Jen slipped up behind him and started tickling him.

"What's going on outside."

"Oh nothing. I asked Charley to move a few plants around by the pool this morning. "

He glanced back toward the closed window then turned around and started tickling her back. He picked her up and threw her over his shoulder, spinning her around, before he tossed her on the bed. He fell down beside her as they laughed together.

Jen suggested Michael shower and get dressed while she started preparing breakfast. When he finally came downstairs, Michael was met with a huge surprise.

Jen and Billy planned a celebration that included family, friends, employees and neighbors. It seemed like everyone in South Georgia showed up to welcome him back.

Half a dozen tables and chairs were set up outside covered with food. A live band was playing country music by the pool and lights were strung up everywhere. There were ribbons, banners and balloons scattered around and large tables covered with every type of food imaginable. Several men stood around a barbeque grill cooking a whole hog.

Kids splashed in the pool while others took pony rides led by Nate and Charley. Guests were singing and dancing, and Michael felt like he really was the prodigal son returning home.

A crowd was gathering around the front of the house, and Michael walked with Jen to discover a brand new Ford pick-up truck with a huge ribbon on the hood.

Michael laughed and said, "What in the world is going on?"

Jen kissed him and said, "It's your welcome home present from me. Welcome back, Darling." She kissed him as the crowd cheered.

The next morning at breakfast, Michael talked to Jen about returning to the Enterprise.

"I can't begin to thank you for stepping in to run things when I... Well, I know you've done a fantastic job, Bill and Walter caught me up on everything, and I've spoken with Sally. They're expecting me to step back in, but I was thinking maybe we could run it together. If that's okay with you. I don't want to get in your way, but I do want to help and be involved again."

Jen smiled, "I would love to work with you as long as you need me, but I should probably start taking it a little easy."

Michael looked puzzled.

"We're having a baby!"

Michael was overjoyed at the news. For the next five months, it was all he could think about or talk about.

There was a noticeable change in his behavior. He was steady and seemed even more at peace than ever. Because of his changed demeanor, those around him at work were happier, too. It seemed that everything was moving calmly but more things were getting accomplished.

Michael was thrilled with how things were going in his life again, and he was full of hope. Even though he had apologized to Jen on many occasions, he felt like there was still more to say.

One Sunday after church, Michael asked Jen to join him in the library, to take a seat and not say anything until he had finished. He sat quietly for a few moments to gather his thoughts, then said, "Jen, I have a sort of confession to make."

He saw Jen stiffen as she expected the worst.

He quickly continued, "It's okay. There's nothing wrong. Everything is find. In fact, everything is perfect."

Jen took a big breath and relaxed in her chair.

Michael continued, "Jen, you remember how things were so perfect. We were so much in love. We had Chip and couldn't have been happier."

Jen realized it was the first time Michael mentioned their son's name since the accident.

Michael continued, "We had friends, money, respect. We had everything a person could want. Then, in an instant, it was gone. We lost everything. I looked at you that horrible morning, and I saw the pain I had caused you. I was going

out of my mind with grief and guilt.
It was too much. I kept hearing
your voice in my mind, day and
night, over and over and over saying
'Oh my god, what have you done!
Michael, you have killed our baby!'
I had to get away from you because I
couldn't stand to see how much I
hurt you. I know I acted horribly to
you. I'm sure it doesn't make sense,
but I didn't leave because I stopped
loving you. I couldn't understand
how you could still love me through
it all, and I left because I loved
you so much."

Jen started to interrupt,
"Michael, don't. Don't do this."

He held his hand up for her to
stop. "Please, Jen. Let me finish. I
saw the pain in your eyes when you
lost your precious baby, yet you
were more concerned with soothing my
pain than worrying about your own.
For me, that made it even worse. I
couldn't understand how you could
still love me after what I had done.
I couldn't get rid of the guilt. I
wanted to talk to you, but I just
couldn't. I had to get away from
you, and I didn't care what happened

to me. I didn't deserve to be okay. I didn't think I could ever come back to you again. When I walked out the door, my heart was broken. I had just left the one person I cared about the most who I absolutely adored. I had lost my reason for living. I started drinking and taking drugs to block you, to block everything, out of my mind. I just didn't want to feel anything anymore. The more I drank the less I felt."

Jen looked at him with tears in her eyes as he went on, "A strange thing happened to me. When I thought I was going to be killed for not being able to pay my debt, I hid in a sewer pipe where they couldn't find me. I stayed there thinking about how far I had fallen. I realized that I had lost more than you, more than myself. I had totally lost God. I abandoned him when I needed him the most, but I thought he was the one who abandoned me. I tried to rely on myself to get through this terrible ordeal. Then something horrible yet strangely

wonderful happened to me. I have a
story to tell you . . ."

Chapter 18: Darkness

to Light

"This is the judgment: the light has come into the world, and people love the darkness rather than the light because their works were evil. But whoever does what is true comes to the light because his works have been carried out in God." John 3:19-21

Michael began telling Jen his incredible story…

As I climbed into the sewer and tried to settle into my hiding place, I heard a voice, but it wasn't coming from outside the sewer. I heard it inside of me, like I heard it with my senses.

The voice said, "When the Son of Man comes in His glory, and all the angels with Him, then He will sit on His glorious throne."

I looked around, but knew I wouldn't see anything in the darkness. The voice said he would separate the people telling one group on his right, "Come, you who are blessed by my Father, inherit the kingdom prepared for you from the foundation of the world."

Then he said to the group on the left, "Depart from me you cursed, into the eternal pit of fire prepared for the devil and his angels. These will go away into eternal punishment, but the righteous into eternal life."

As I sat huddled in the sewer pipe, I felt myself descending into an endless, black pit. I could feel an emptiness around me, then I realized the emptiness was not just around me, it was inside me. I couldn't see in the darkness, but I could hear voices of people all around, screaming and howling in terrifying pain. I could hear crying, moaning, wailing from souls in intense suffering agony. I felt myself being pulled down, down into a raging inferno as the flames from the fire were lapping at me. Strangely, they didn't burn me, and I didn't feel heat or pain.

All around me, there was a putrid odor that reeked of sulfuric acid and rotten eggs. It was so horrendous, I felt like I was going to vomit.

As I sank deeper into the pit, I started seeing images of hideous, incongruously distorted faces, some floating, some flying around me. They would suddenly dart at me as though they wanted to devour me, continually appearing then disappearing into the darkness.

As I sank deeper, there were huge, terrifying animals, like grotesque creatures that would charge at me bearing sharp, pointy teeth. The wind howled mournfully, and there was screaming all around me. It sounded like hundreds of people were being tortured.

As all this was going on around me, I felt a sudden, terrifying loss, like something inside of me was dying. There aren't words to describe it.

I continued to descend further and saw hideous half human, half goat-like beings thrashing around aimlessly, clawing and bumping into each other. They would stumble and fall, crawling around, screaming then starting the process over and over.

I began falling into the middle of an intense volcanic fire with millions of suffering people biting and clawing at each other trying to get out of the ghastly flames leaping all around them.

In the midst of this horror, I began to realize that I had lost everything, my hope, my faith, my love. I had become a vacuous, empty shell.

As I huddled in the chaos, with the tornadic wind howling all around me in this bottomless chasm, I saw through the darkness a flickering light like the flame on a candle. I wondered why the light didn't blow out.

I continued to stare at the flame, and a terrifying realization covered me. I knew if the light went out, I would never return, but return to what? I would never return to life. I would never leave this ghastly abyss of hell.

Immersed in this chaos, I wondered how there could be anything redeeming left of me. The horrors happening around me were everywhere, forever, for all eternity. I didn't feel pain, but I sensed the fear and hatred that surrounded me as I suddenly remembered the first time I opened the Bible. It was when you asked me to read the Gospel of John, and I read a few lines for no other reason than to impress you.

One line caught my attention. I read it over and over, but I didn't really understand what it meant at the time. The line went something like, "In Him was life and the life was the light of men. The light shines in the darkness, and the darkness has not overcome it."

I then realized that no matter how horrible my life had become and even though I had given up on myself, the light of the candle would never go out because that light was God's unconditional, merciful and divine love for me...for all of us.

Unexpectedly, I felt hope and reassurance that everything would be alright. The light from the candle grew brighter, and I became aware that the light was coming from outside the sewer pipe. After so many agonizing months of despair, I experienced this wonderful sensation of exaltation as I crawled out of my hiding place and into the warmth and light of the sun.

I sank down to my knees in the middle of the human waste and filth and thanked the Lord for delivering me from damnation. I thanked him for the blessings he gives us every day that we simply take for granted. I thanked him for His unceasing love.

For the first time in my life, I looked around and truly saw and appreciated the beauty of the gifts He has given us to enjoy on this earth while we are on our journey back to Him. It was like I could see for the first time the sunlight streaming through the branches of the trees, birds singing, the aroma of flowers in bloom, all displaying God's love for us.

I knew then that if I could just make it to Billy's, he would help me get back from this nightmare. Well, you know the rest. Soon after that, he brought me home.

"Michael, that is incredible. I don't know what to say. It really does sound like a horrible nightmare."

Michael solemnly replied, "It was like being in a nightmare where you want to wake up but you can't. Only, this was real. It was as real as the two of us sitting here together. I know for certain that I descended to a place where God gave me a glimpse into hell. By His grace, he brought me back. I don't know why. I just know it happened."

The two of them sat quietly together while the significance of his story sank in, then Jen finally said, "Why on earth didn't you tell me about this months ago? We've spent countless hours talking about so much, sharing our inner most thoughts and feelings."

"I wanted to have it clear in my head. I felt extremely confused after so much time on drugs and alcohol, and I wanted to be sure it wasn't just some crazy hallucination. It had to be clear in my own mind before I told you or anyone else."

Michael continued, "I've searched my heart and soul and prayed about it every day. I believe the Holy Spirit is continually speaking to me saying, 'Remember the word of Jesus: I AM the Christ, the Son of the Living God; I AM, who was crucified on the cross to atone for man's sins; I AM the resurrection and the life. Whoever believes in me, though he die, yet shall he live.' I finally understand the reference to life, light and darkness. Jesus as the light brings to this dark world true knowledge, moral purity and the light that shows the very presence of God."

Later that night, as Michael lay in bed staring up at the ceiling, he whispered to Jen, "Sweetheart, after all I put you through, all the pain and heartache I caused you, why didn't you ever divorce me?"

"Actually, Michael, there are many reasons. The first and most important reason is that I made a vow to you and to God.

"The second reason is my belief that when two people marry, they become one flesh. It's like we each had a glass of water. Yours was colored yellow and mine blue. When we each poured our colors together into a third glass, they combined to make green. Our separate water didn't change in substance, but it created a new one.

"The third reason is simple. I love you.

"And the forth reason goes back to the first time we met at the Brighton Academy stadium. Do you remember?"

Michael smiled and answered, "Yes. When I was struggling and needed help, you said you would always be there for me and never leave me."

Jen said, "That's right. Whenever you need me, I will always be there for you. I will be at your side no matter what."

Michael shook his head, smiled and thought… I will never understand this girl!

Chapter 19: Angels

"For this very night there stood before me an angel of the God to whom I belong and whom I worship." Acts 27:23

As Job's fortunes were returned to him because of his faithfulness, so were the treasures of Michael and Jen. Their home was filled with the laughter and squeals of happy children.

Their daughter Elizabeth, now six, had black hair and dark blue-green eyes like her mother. She loved animals and spent countless hours with the horses. Her favorite activity was riding her pony, Gidget, out to Lonesome Pine with her mother and picking wildflowers in the field.

Little Billy, at four years old, had the same coloring as his sister and followed her everywhere. People often thought they were twins. He loved to have stories read to him and could most often be found stretched out on the library sofa with a picture book or pretending to read to himself from one of the many leather bound books from the shelves.

The biggest personality came in the form of the smallest member of the family. Two year old Tommy, named for Jen's father, looked most like Michael with blonde hair and blue eyes. He was into everything and very inquisitive, always asking questions with his favorite word being "why." He followed his father everywhere, and the older children called him Daddy's shadow.

Michael and Jen felt immensely blessed with their healthy and beautiful children and the continued success of the Enterprise and Farm activities. In spite of Bill Baxter's previous warning about changing the structure of business operations, profits soared and employees were extremely happy and loyal.

One evening, Michael was working late on a contract at the office and missed the family dinner invitation at the Prescotts' house.

They offered to bring him a plate but with Jen's hands full with three kids, he insisted on stopping at the diner on the way home so she wouldn't have to bother.

He finished working around 8:30, locked up the office and headed down the street for dinner. He was running through the contract in his head, making sure he had taken care of all the necessary items before passing it on to the legal department to finalize. A light rain started to fall, so Michael picked up the pace, when a man, ragged and dirty, suddenly appeared from an alley.

Michael was startled when the vagrant said, "Mister, could you spare a few dollars? I'm terribly hungry."

He watched the man who was obviously homeless and living on the street. With long, unruly hair, bushy eyebrows and a scraggly beard, the man was short and thin and wore tattered clothes. Michael stared at him as a wave of familiarity came over him. This man was him 10 years ago.

Most people would have crossed over to the other side of the street or possibly given a few dollars to the man out of guilt, but Michael knew what it was like to be hungry, to hope for a few scraps of food to fill his stomach. His last meal was probably from a dumpster.

This destitute man likely sought shelter in abandoned buildings or under bridges as Michael had years ago. He wasn't worried about the man becoming violent. There was something unusual and kind in his expression.

When Michael didn't reply, the man tried again, "Hey, Mister. Any spare change?"

Awakened from his daze, Michael said, "Oh, I'm sorry. I was thinking about something that happened to me years ago. Look, I'm going into the diner. Would you join me for dinner?"

The man seemed surprised by the invitation, but not wanting to miss the chance to eat, agreed to accompany him.

When they entered the crowded restaurant, everyone turned to look at them. Some quickly turned away, not wanting to acknowledge the condition of this man. Others stared in disgust, realizing they would be dining a few tables away from someone in ragged, smelly clothes.

The waitress approached their table, addressing only Michael.

"Can I get you something to drink?"

"To start with, we would like two menus. I'll have a large glass of milk, and he'll have the same."

Michael originally intended to stop in for a quick burger and piece of apple pie before heading home, but when the waitress returned, Michael said, "I would like the turkey and dressing special with rice, sweet potatoes and lots of gravy. Afterward, I want a piece of apple pie, heated, with ice cream."

The waitress, still looking annoyed, pointed her pencil at Michael's guest and said, "What about him?"

"Bring him the same thing."

While they waited for their food to arrive, Michael asked the man about his life and how he ended up on the street.

The man sadly told the story. "My wife and baby were killed in an auto accident five years ago. I guess I couldn't get over it. I appreciate the food, but I don't really want to talk about it."

Michael said he understood and was extremely sorry for his loss. As he stared at the man's face, he realized what was so unique about him. His eyes, though sorrowful, were warm and penetrating. They were also the most unusual shade of light brown he had ever seen.

Michael nibbled at the fare on his plate, but the homeless man devoured every bite, including both slices of apple pie. When he finished, he ran the napkin over his mouth and simply said, "Thank you, Mister."

Michael paid for their dinner and requested a box for leftovers. As they walked back out into the drizzle, Michael held out his hand with the food and said, "Here, please take this. I won't eat it. By the way, what is your name?"

The man replied, "Its Tayler with an e-r."

"Very glad to meet you, Tayler with an e-r. I hope to see you again."

The man looked at Michael with his penetrating eyes and said, "Oh, you will Michael."

Tayler turned away and without looking, stepped into the street. Instinctively, Michael quickly glanced both ways checking for cars. When he turned back to say goodnight to Tayler, he was gone. He simply vanished.

"That's impossible!" Michael said out loud.

He was stunned knowing that the man could not just disappear. He should only have reached the center of the street in the time it took Michael to look around for oncoming traffic.

Michael walked out in the street, turning around and glancing in all directions saying, "He's gone! He's gone!"

Two elderly women were walking down the street and quickly stepped closer to the buildings to avoid him as they hurried on their way. It started to rain harder, and they opened their umbrellas. Michael ran past, startling them, knowing he must look insane as the rain came down even harder.

He suddenly stopped in the middle of the sidewalk and said, "He called me Michael. I never told him my name."

Drenched and muddled, Michael drove home scanning the streets and sidewalks as he made his way through town hoping to catch a glimpse of Tayler. His drive took him past the old Madison Hotel which had been abandoned for years. He wondered if Tayler ever slept there. The city had tried on several occasions to have the building condemned and torn down, but they were met with resistance from the Historical Society every time. The Society hoped to obtain funding to eventually restore the 150 year old building to its original glory, but for now, it was plastered with No Trespassing signs and danger warnings.

Michael drove up the driveway just as Jen was returning from dinner with her parents. He helped her carry in the sleepy children and asked her about their night.

Jen was concerned. "You know Dad is on the school board. He said they are getting a lot of complaints from worried parents about the growing number of homeless people in town. Apparently, there have been quite a few incidents where vagrants have asked for money, and people in town are afraid and feeling threatened. Of course, dad has a different opinion and a few people actually took his side that mostly the homeless around town want to be left alone and need to be able to live, too. Others in the meeting said the homeless should be rounded up and put someplace away from town. The conversation went on and on without anything ever coming of it."

Michael went to the kitchen and said, "Do we have anything for dessert?"

Jen teased, "You mean, you didn't get your usual slice of pie with ice cream from the diner? I figured that was the real reason you went."

"Actually, I was on my way to the diner when I met a man on the street who stopped me and asked for some money for food. He said he was hungry, so I invited him to eat with me. I gave him my dessert."

Michael told Jen the whole story, including how the man seemed to disappear into the rain. When he finished, he said, "You may think I'm crazy, but I know I didn't tell him my name. Yet, somehow, he knew me. I think I had dinner with an angel."

"Michael, is it possible he remembered you from the street? You were there for a long time."

Michael said, "I was off the street for several years before his wife and child died, so he couldn't possibly have known me. And how do you explain him vanishing before my eyes?"

"I can't explain it, but there has to be a reason you met him."

That night, Michael slept very little and was restless throughout the long night. Jen was concerned when he woke her up repeatedly during the night, and she asked what was bothering him so much.

"I'm sorry, Jen. I've got a few things weighing heavily on my mind. I can't stop thinking about the homeless issue in town and the concerns of the people at the meeting. I want to do something to help. I think you're right, there was a reason I met Tayler tonight. There was also a reason Tom brought up the issue over dinner. Can you come to my office around 10 in the morning?"

"Sure, I'll be there, but what's going on?"

"I'm not sure myself, but I'll know by 10."

When Michael arrived at the office, he asked Sally to call an urgent meeting with the executive staff in the large conference room at 10. Everyone needed to attend and arrive on time. He also asked Sally to be there. Jen arrived and went straight to the conference room followed by Michael who greeted the staff already in attendance.

"I know you're wondering what this meeting is all about, so I'll quickly get to the point. I'm sure you're all familiar with the abandoned Madison Hotel.

"My plan is for us to purchase the old hotel, renovate it, designing rooms to take in a significant number of people off the street. I want to set up a program that not only houses the homeless but also feeds them, offers counseling services, job training and rehabilitation.

"We need to hire a staff consisting of administrators, maintenance personnel, kitchen help, etc. with doctors and psychiatrists who make regular visits. It'll be similar to a regular hotel except the guests don't pay, and the services we offer are unique. Well, I guess it's not like a regular hotel at all."

Michael stopped, took a deep breath and said, "So now, I need to hear from you the reasons why this plan won't work."

The responses were immediate:

"It will cost a fortune."

"How would we recover our investment?"

"We'll never get this past planning and zoning."

"The Historical Society will never agree to it."

"Who covers salaries and ongoing expenses?"

"What is the timeline getting this off the ground?"

"Who would actually own the property?"

Jen spoke up, "Well, I can answer the question of who owns the property. We do." Everyone in the room turned toward Jen as she continued, "I was doing some research at the courthouse and came across documents showing the title is held by Tillman Bank."

Michael smiled and said, "Okay, we have that answered, so one problem is already solved. Come on guys, I can think of a lot more reasons why we should not do this, but let me give you the reasons we should. The building, as it now stands, is an eyesore to the downtown area, and the city has been trying for years to demolish it. The homeless are a problem for downtown business workers and shoppers. Tourism has dropped significantly, and we can't attract conventions to the area. The chamber is convinced vagrants are causing a public nuisance and an economic hardship.

"Ladies and gentlemen, we can get these people off the streets and give them a decent place to live. We can help with their recovery and hopeful reintegration into society. If we give them an opportunity for rehabilitation, we can make a significant difference.

"As most of you know, I have first-hand experience with the horrors of life on the streets. I know there are many people who, with a little help, can start to get their lives back on track and return to a meaningful existence.

One of the executives asked, "Michael, is your interest in this project merely because of your personal experiences."

Michael replied, "No, I really don't think so. In fact, I've tried very hard to put that period of time behind me. I haven't thought about it in years. A few days ago, however, I had dinner with a man who opened my eyes to an important reality. Since then, I haven't been able to stop thinking about our duty to 'feed the hungry, clothe the naked, give shelter to the homeless, give aid to the sick.'"

Bill Baxter spoke up, "Michael, I understand why you feel so passionately about this, but you haven't said how we are going to pay for it all. It's going to be extremely expensive to start up and maintain."

Michael replied, "First, we'll start with the Tillman Foundation. We already have money in our budget for charitable contributions. We can shift things around and allocate money for this project without totally depleting our other donations.

"Most local businesses and large corporations earmark money annually for charitable causes. Why not this one? Also, I know many wealthy families around the state who would likely get behind an endeavor like ours, and we haven't even begun to research funds available through Federal, State and Local grants and endowments.

Michael asked, "Before we adjourn, are there any more questions?" The meeting ended and everyone returned to work except for Jen, Sally Bill and Walter.

Michael had a few final instructions for his closest and most trusted advisors.

"Sally, will you please call the community center and reserve their largest meeting room for two weeks from Thursday? Next, I need you to call the Governor's office and request a private meeting between the Governor and myself at his earliest convenience. I will clear my schedule to drive up to Atlanta. I'll just need a few hours notice. Please stress the urgency for us to meet as quickly as possible, but I will only need about an hour of his time. I would also like to coordinate a meeting with the Secretary of State while I'm in Atlanta."

"Definitely. I'll get right on it."

"Walter, if you've still got connections with the local folks, will you please arrange a meeting with the City Manager and the Finance Administrator?"

"Sure. Those guys owe me a few favors. I'll call them today and set something up."

"If you and Bill will reach out to our business contacts who have power and influence and try to get them behind this project with us, that would be a great help. Call everyone you can think of in South Georgia and around the state, and lets get some serious support on this.

"Jen, I want you to start working with our Public Relations department on detail for the newspaper. Get with the radio and TV stations around the state to start sharing information and providing updates on our progress. We may get some foundation donations as well."

From that first meeting, an idea that grew from a chance

encounter on a rainy night came a
step closer to becoming a reality.

Chapter 20: The Power of Love

"But God, being rich in mercy, because of the great love with which he loved us, even when we were dead in our trespasses, made us alive in Christ, by grace you have been saved." Ephesians 2:4

The office was buzzing as everyone worked diligently on their assigned projects. The next morning, Sally entered Michael's office with an update.

"The large meeting room at the community center is booked as you requested for two weeks from tomorrow, and the city administrators said they would be happy to meet with you here today at 2:00. I reserved the small conference room for you, and I'll have a fresh pot of coffee ready when they arrive. I heard back from the Governor, and he is available on Monday morning at 9:30. The Secretary of State said he would move a few things around so he is free at 11:00. I reserved a room for you at the Georgian Terrace Hotel on Sunday night, so you can take your time getting there this weekend."

"Good work, Sally. I don't know what I'd do without you."

With a smile, Sally turned to leave and said, "A raise would be nice."

Michael laughed and pointed at the door. "Out! Out!"

On Monday morning, Michael was greeted by the Governor's administrative assistant, Pam, who announced his arrival. When Michael was escorted into the office, the Governor welcomed him.

"Good morning, Michael. It's nice to see you again."

"It's nice to see you, too, Governor."

"Please call me Jack."

Pam brought in a pot of coffee and an elaborate breakfast as the men took a seat at the table.

"I have a real South Georgia breakfast for you, Michael. I hope you enjoy it. We have scrambled eggs, grits, hoe cakes, may-haw jelly and the best country sausage you have ever tasted. A friend of mine makes it himself. He's from down in your part of the state in Moultrie, I think. His name is Bob Davis."

"It's Ben. Ben Davis. As a matter of fact, I went quail hunting at his place last year. He gave me ten pounds of sausage, and you're right, it is the best I have ever tasted."

Jack said, "He only gave me five pounds."

Michael smiled, "Yes, but he helped get you elected."

"That's right. And I can't thank you enough for your support. Having the Tillman Enterprise behind me helped deliver most of South Georgia. I don't think I'd be Governor today without it."

"I'm glad you realize that, Jack."

Michael spent the next hour talking to the Governor about his plan for renovating the Madison Hotel and creating a safe environment for the rehabilitation of the homeless population in that area.

"Michael, are you sure you're not biting off more than you can chew?"

"Jack, I really don't think so. Not with your support and support from the government. I am also hoping to pull in support from hundreds of wealthy and influential people around the state."

The Governor said, "This could be a potentially risky political venture for me to support."

"Jack, there will be a tremendous amount of public relations and marketing involved. If you have any further political aspirations, you may need this project. If it takes off, it could spread throughout the country. You need to get behind this and get your name associated with it on the ground floor."

"Michael, how much support do you need?"

Michael leaned forward and said, "To start, two million dollars."

"I can't get that kind of money."

"Jack, you can get it out of your state slush fund. I'm going to ask the Secretary of State to consider including it in the state budget after I ask for his upfront support. "

The Governor thought for a few seconds and replied, "Alright Michael. You have your two million as long as you can get the necessary approvals to get this thing off the ground, but if you think you're going to get any support from the Secretary of State, you're seriously mistaken. If I remember correctly, you vigorously campaigned against him in the last election. You did everything you could to get him defeated. What makes you think you can get him to support your project? I know for a fact that he isn't running again, and without political aspirations, he has no other reason to help you."

Michael smiled at the Governor and said, "Oh ye of little faith, watch and see what can happen when the Holy Spirit gets involved."

Michael thanked the Governor for his time and headed to his next meeting with the Secretary of State, but he did not receive the same cordial reception.

"Good morning, Mr. Tillman. I don't have much time. What can I do for you?"

Michael shared his ideas and the tremendous support he had received already, making sure to stress the backing he recently gained from the Governor.

"Mr. Tillman, tell me why I should support your project? Remember, you and I are on opposite sides of the political fence, and you were quite vocal in your opposition to me in the last primary election."

Michael said, "This is not a political project, it's a humanitarian one. You are quite outspoken in your faith, and it is well known that you are a Christian man."

"Yes, a devout Christian."

"Then you are familiar with Matthew 25:35-36: 'For I was hungry and you gave me food; I was thirsty and you gave me drink; I was a stranger and you welcomed me; I was naked and you clothed me; I was sick and you visited me.'"

The Secretary of State was quiet for a minute as he thought about what Michael had just said.

"Say no more, Michael. I will submit a request for five million dollars and will work toward getting long term funding added to the state budget. Good luck to you."

The next two weeks flew by as details continued to be worked out, and every major hurdle was overcome. The day of Michael's public meeting arrived. He and Jen pulled into the community center and were stunned to see the local support.

Jen grabbed Michael's arm and said, "Oh my! There must be at least a hundred cars and look at all the buses!"

Michael was shocked, "There must be over 300 people here!"

They were met by the community center director when they entered the building and were informed that the large conference room would not hold the crowd, so she moved their meeting to the auditorium. As Michael and Jen entered, they were greeted with a standing ovation.

Michael acknowledged the welcome and asked the audience to remain standing for a blessing over the proceedings, and he then spent the next hour talking about the project and sharing the support they had received from the Governor and Secretary of State as well as numerous foundations and individuals. He shared architectural renderings of the renovation and the initial estimates and ongoing budgets for the project.

After providing the project details, he opened the meeting up for questions. The first inquiry pertained to the administrative duties of the Foundation and the Madison Facility.

Michael explained there would be separate board of directors for each, with the Foundation being primarily responsible for fundraising and financial planning while the Facility would be solely involved with the day to day operations and supervision of the individuals in rehabilitation.

The next question related to the number of people who would be housed at the facility and the amount of supervision they would receive.

"First of all, we will refer to these individuals as 'trainees'. We want them to maintain their dignity, and this seems like the best approach. The first year, we would like to have fifty trainees with each having a private room. They will be responsible for the care and cleanliness of their personal space as well as having various jobs either within the facility or in the community. We will also offer job training and college classes at VSU. As you know, our goal is to get them ready to return to the community as contributing members of society."

Michael answered questions for the next hour and a half when a community member asked, "Why is the Foundation under the Tillman umbrella? You are asking a lot of people for money, and it seems like this should be separate from your family enterprises."

"Thank you for the question, and you're exactly right. This project definitely stands alone and will not be under the Tillman name. I believe we should call it the Tayler Foundation. After all, it was his idea. He planned and organized the project from the beginning and will make sure it is completed according to God's will."

Jen jumped up and shouted, "Yes! The Tayler Foundation!" She was immediately embarrassed and, with a red face, sat back down.

Michael said with a laugh, "You'll have to excuse my beautiful wife. She gets a little over enthusiastic sometimes!"

He continued, "Most of you knew my grandfather. He was a hard man to deal with in business, but you could always bank on the fact that his word was his bond. I think we can all agree with that. I have run the Enterprise for many years, and although I have a different approach than my grandfather, I hope you all know that my word is my bond as well, and today I give you my solemn word, this proposed endeavor will be a reality within two years.

"Ladies and Gentlemen, I am so glad you all came today, and I appreciate your support. Before we adjourn, I would like to leave you with this teaching from Jesus found in 1 John 3:21-24: 'Beloved, if our heart does not condemn us, we have confidence before God and whatever we ask we receive from Him because we keep His commandments and do what pleases Him. And this is His commandment, that we believe in the name of His Son, Jesus Christ, and love one another just as He has commanded us. Whoever keeps His commandments abides in God and God in him. And by this we know that He abides in us, by the Spirit whom He has given us."

Michael concluded by saying, "I believe this more than I believe anything else in the world. Thank you and God bless and keep you safe."

True to his word, Michael, with the help of countless friends and supporters around the state, followed through with his promise to make the Madison Hotel and Tayler Foundation a reality. Through their tireless efforts, the program far exceeded expectations and was such a tremendous success that many similar facilities opened in different cities around the country as a result.

Nationwide, these facilities had various levels of success and were responsible for thousands of lives being rehabilitated. Numerous individuals entered the program and received the help they needed to lead productive lives again.

By far, the most successful facility was the original Madison Hotel. After the renovations were complete, the first fifty trainees entered the program. A few dropped out, but the majority of the people who began the program received the help they needed and were able to move out of the facility and find full time employment.

They continued to be monitored and supported medically and psychologically and were tested for drugs and alcohol. If they ever needed help, it was readily available to them. As soon as one person was able to leave, their spot was quickly filled by a new trainee until the facility reached its maximum capacity.

At dinner one night, Michael and Jen were discussing the latest improvements to the facility.

Jen said, "Michael, the PR Department receives calls every day asking for information about the Tayler Foundation. They are so overwhelmed, we may have to hire someone in that department just to answer the phone. They're also getting a lot of calls from newspapers and TV stations wanting to interview you."

Michael laughed, "Jen, that's why I put you in charge of Public Relations. You can answer their questions, so go out and Public Relate!"

Jen rolled her eyes as she got up to answer the phone.

"Yes, this is she. Who did you say you were with? Really? This isn't a joke? Yes. Definitely. I'll tell him."

Jen hung up the phone and said, "Michael, that was a representative of the Georgia Man of the Year selection committee. You are one of five men nominated for the award this year!"

Michael said, "Are you kidding me? Who in their right mind would nominate me for such a thing?"

The next morning after Michael left for work, the children were sitting around the table having breakfast when Jen said to them, "Kids, you should be very proud of your father. He is the most amazing and unbelievable person I have ever known."

Elizabeth looked up from her plate and said, "Oh, yea, Mom. Is he like famous or something?"

Billy chimed in, "No, he's not famous. He's just Dad."

Tommy wasn't going to be left out, "My daddy is to famous. He's the most famous person in the world, ain't he, Mom?"

Jen smiled, "Isn't he Tommy, not ain't he."

Tommy stuck his tongue out at his older siblings.

A month later, the results were tallied, and Michael Tillman was selected Georgia's new Man of the Year. He was touched by the gesture and humbled to be recognized for the efforts that so many people had been a part of as well.

The day of the presentation arrived, and the Tillmans spent the afternoon participating in their favorite pastime, riding horses as a family out to Lonesome Pine for a picnic. As the children were throwing stones into the lake, Michael and Jen sat on a blanket and talked.

Michael said, "You know, Jen, sometimes I really do feel like Job. When I was a little boy, I lost my parents. Several years later, I lost Matty who was like a mother to me and the only person I felt truly cared about me at the time. We lost Chip in the horrible accident, then I lost my wonderful wife who I adored. I lost my job at the

Enterprise, my home, my friends, my self-respect and ended up hiding in a sewer pipe where I experienced the torment of Hell, but look where we are now. I feel truly blessed."

Jen whispered, "It seems overwhelming, but God doesn't make mistakes. If this is the journey God had planned for you then you can be sure He will give back twice what he took away if you are true to Him and trust Him."

"Throughout our lives together, I have caused you so much pain and heartache. The one person I loved the most in the world I hurt the most. You always said you would never leave me and you never have. But more than that, Jen, you reached my soul and taught me to love and about the love of Jesus. You showed me how to give my life to Him so that one day I will live in the glory of God for eternity."

The Tillmans attended the award ceremony together that night surrounded by family and friends. Michael appreciated the recognition but was happiest knowing to his family, he would forever strive to be Husband and Dad of the Year and faithful to whatever God had in store for him.

A huge group gathered at The Farm after the ceremony ended to continue the celebration. Michel and Jen greeted guests and mingled in the crowd. Later in the evening, as Michael stepped out onto the patio alone, he glanced across the pool and saw a man standing on the other side facing away from him. He didn't recognize him at first, but there was something familiar about him. As the man turned toward him, Michael recognized the unique color of his eyes...light brown.

Michael ran over to him, and with tears in his eyes, hugged the man who was responsible for transforming countless lives. Tayler put his hand on Michael's shoulder and said, "'Well done, good and faithful servant' (Matt 25:23).

"Whether you are blessed with talent, wealth, knowledge or time, it is expected that we use these gifts well to glorify God and benefit others. You have done these things."

'For unto whomever much is given, of him shall much be required.'" (Luke 12:48)

Michael, slowly recovering from the surprise of seeing Tayler so unexpectedly again said, "Wait here. There is someone I want you to meet! Don't go anywhere!"

Michael rushed back into the house and found Jen talking with a group of friends. "Please excuse her for just a second. I really need to borrow her."

As he quickly led her out of the house, Jen said, "Michael, what's going on? I was in the middle of a conversation when you pulled me away."

Michael stammered, "I am so sorry. You aren't going to believe who's here! Come on! Tayler is outside by the pool."

They ran outside together, but when they gazed across the pool, Tayler was gone.

THE END

Epilogue

This is the end of the story but not
the end of Michael and Jen who will
live on in the hearts and memories
of those who knew and loved them. I
hope you enjoyed the story.

Acknowledgements

I had the pleasure, fun and enjoyment of writing this book, and I would be remiss if I didn't thank my grandson, Michael, for organizing the format and giving the book life. More especially, I want to thank Elizabeth for her endless hours of proof reading and typing the entire book. It could not have been completed without her assistance. God bless Michael and Elizabeth.

Jimmy Campagna

Made in the USA
Columbia, SC
21 July 2017